8/09

D0950021

Match Wits with Super Sleuth Nancy Drew!

Collect the Original
Nancy Drew Mystery Stories
by Carolyn Keene

Available in Hardcover!

Celebrate 60 Years with the World's Best Detective!

THE CLUE OF THE BROKEN LOCKET

NANCY DREW and her friends are plunged into a network of strange events when they visit Misty Lake. The very night they arrive, they meet pretty, red-haired Cecily Curtis, who seeks Nancy's help in solving two mysteries: one concerning Cecily's fiancé, Niko Van Dyke, a popular singer who believes that his record company is cheating him of royalty payments; the other, involving a family treasure hidden before the start of the Civil War—Cecily's only clue being half of a gold locket.

Nancy's investigations lead her to Pudding Stone Lodge, where the sinister Driscoll family lives. Elusive humming noises, a flashing light in the attic of the lodge, the periodic apparition of an excursion launch which had sunk in Misty Lake years ago, and the fleeting appearances of a frightened girl who strongly resembles Cecily give Nancy plenty of opportunity to test her sleuthing skills.

Braving a series of dangerous situations and discouraging developments, the alert young detective perseveres in her attempts to solve both mysteries and reveal the astounding secrets of Pudding Stone Lodge.

"She's here somewhere!"

NANCY DREW MYSTERY STORIES®

The Clue of the Broken Locket

BY CAROLYN KEENE

GROSSET & DUNLAP
Publishers • New York
A member of The Putnam & Grosset Group

PRINTED ON RECYCLED PAPER

Acknowledgement is made to Mildred Wirt Benson, who writing under the pen name
Carolyn Keene, wrote the original NANCY DREW books.

Contents

CHAPTER I

Key to a Mystery

As Nancy Drew seated herself at the breakfast table, she noticed a door key beside her plate. The attractive titian-haired girl looked up in surprise at her father, who had just pulled out his own chair.

"Is this for me?" she asked the tall, handsome attorney.

He smiled. "Nancy, that may be a key to a mystery."

"In our house? Or somewhere here in River Heights?"

Carson Drew shook his head. "At a cabin on Misty Lake, in Maryland. Would you like to go there and find out what has frightened a certain Mr. Winch?"

Nancy's blue eyes sparkled. The eighteen-year-old girl had already solved many mysteries for her father and at once was eager to take on a new one. She begged to hear more about it.

"I have a client," Mr. Drew began, "by the name of Lawrence Baker, who owns a summer cottage on Misty Lake. He is now in Europe. Before leaving, he arranged to rent his place for two weeks to a young woman from New Orleans, Cecily Curtis. Mr. Baker says she has an interesting story but did not tell me what it was. He asked if I would draw up the rent agreement." Mr. Drew paused, his eyes twinkling.

"Oh, Dad!" Nancy laughed. "Please! Don't keep me in suspense!"

"Well, Miss Curtis was to pick up this key to the cottage from Henry Winch, who had agreed to keep an eye on the place. I understand he is quite a character—knows everyone and tells wonderful stories. He lives near there the year round in the rear of his small shop where he sells confectionery and fish bait!"

Nancy chuckled. "He does sound like a colorful character. Confectionery and bait make quite a combination!"

Her father explained that since it was the middle of September, there would probably be few vacationers at the lake. "I can't imagine why Cecily Curtis wants to stay there. If you meet her, Nancy, perhaps you can find out."

"I'm all set to go!" Nancy said eagerly. "Tell

me more about Henry Winch and why he's so frightened."

"During the summer he rents out boats, as well as selling bait and candy. In winter he stores boats for the summer residents, is caretaker for their cottages, and does odd jobs for the villagers. He sent me this key to the Baker place, along with a note, but gave no hint as to *what* had frightened him. Look here."

The attorney reached into his pocket and brought out a plain piece of paper. He handed it to Nancy. The note read:

Hire somebody else. I'm scared.
H. Winch

"This is all he wrote?" Nancy asked.

"Yes. Here's the problem. Cecily Curtis is to arrive at Misty Lake late tomorrow evening, but Mr. Winch apparently wants nothing to do with the cottage. I can't leave at the moment, so I thought you could drive down there with the key and open the cabin for Miss Curtis. I don't want you to go alone, though."

"Maybe Bess and George can join me!"

George Fayne and her cousin Bess Marvin had been friends of Nancy's for a long time. The three had shared many exciting adventures when mysteries had come their way. Bess had often remarked that Nancy was like honey with "the mystery bees swarming around her all the time."

This was true from the time she had helped her father solve *The Secret of the Old Clock* to her most recent challenge, deciphering *The Password to Larkspur Lane.*

Nancy hurried to the telephone and called the two girls. Fortunately, neither of them had special dates for the next few days and would be able to accompany Nancy. It was arranged that the trio would leave early that afternoon and drive at least partway to the lake.

By the time Nancy came back to the table, the Drews' motherly housekeeper was there and had already heard about Nancy's latest plans. Hannah Gruen had lived with the Drews since Nancy was three, when her mother had died. Nancy adored Hannah, who always did a great deal of worrying about her when she was working on a mystery.

"Is it okay with the girls?" Mr. Drew asked.

Nancy nodded. "George is keen about the idea."

"I'd expect that," Mr. Drew commented. "She's very level-headed and sensible." He chuckled. "I'll bet Bess is a little hesitant, though."

"Right," said Nancy, and smiled. "Bess always worries about the possibility of running into danger, but she's one of the world's best sports when the necessity arises."

Presently Mr. Drew said that he must hurry

off to his office. He kissed Nancy and wished her luck. "I believe there's a nice guest house in the village of Misty Lake, about a mile from the water. You might stay there."

By two o'clock Nancy was packed and on her way to pick up Bess and George. First she stopped at the Marvin home and Bess came out carrying a suitcase. She was a very pretty blonde, inclined to be overweight. "Hi, Nance! I'm glad you put the top of your convertible down. It's a gorgeous day."

A few minutes later Nancy stopped for George Fayne. The slim, short-haired brunette with the boy's name came out of the house, vigorously swinging a small suitcase. She tossed it into the rear seat and climbed into the front beside the other two.

After greetings, she said, "Now, Nancy, give us the details on this case we're going to solve."

"First of all, there's a frightened caretaker," Nancy began, and quickly brought her friends up to date. Suddenly one of Bess's turquoise earrings fell into her lap.

"Oh, this old earring makes me so mad. It's always falling off."

"Why don't you tighten it?" George asked. She was apt to be impatient with her very feminine cousin. Bess adjusted the screw and slipped the earring back on.

Late in the afternoon the girls stopped at a motel for dinner and overnight. The following day, they continued on to Misty Lake. In the afternoon, as they came closer to their destination, the three began to do a lot of guessing about Mr. Winch and Cecily Curtis. Finally George declared that their theories probably were one hundred percent wrong.

Bess changed the subject by saying, "We don't know a thing about how good the food is in Misty Lake. Why don't we stop for an early supper?"

This was agreed upon and the girls began to watch for likely places. On the outskirts of a town called Brookville they came to an attractive restaurant, the White Mill. It was a remodeled mill, with a stream underneath part of it.

"This is charming," said Bess. "And look! The sign says fresh broiled lobster. Mmm!"

"That sounds good to me too," Nancy remarked.

She parked the car and the three girls went inside. A pleasant waitress who spoke in a soft drawl seated them and took their orders. "There'll be a twenty-minute wait for the lobster," she said. "Why don't you all go out and walk around the garden, then cross the bridge into the woods? It's really very lovely."

Nancy and her friends took the waitress's suggestion and went out the side door, which led into the garden. There was a profusion of many colors and varieties of chrysanthemums, late-blooming roses, and petunias. A path through the center of the garden led directly to a rustic white-painted bridge over a rushing stream.

"The bridge is quaint, but it looks rickety," said Bess.

"Oh, come on," George urged.

The girls, however, carefully crossed the bridge one by one and entered the woods.

Bess took a deep breath. "This smells heavenly!" she said in almost a whisper, as if she did not want to disturb any of the wildlife.

As the three friends advanced, they suddenly became aware of a young couple seated on a fallen log a little distance away. The girl, who had curly red hair, had a troubled look on her pretty face. Her fair-haired companion seemed vaguely familiar to the girls, but they were sure they had not met him. The couple, engrossed in conversation, did not notice the newcomers.

Nancy and the cousins quietly turned in another direction. Just as they were out of sight of the couple, the red-haired girl cried out, "Why can't you understand? I don't want to get married with a lawsuit hanging over our heads!"

As Nancy and her friends glanced at one another, the boy shouted, "That's not the real reason! It's the iron bird that's coming between us! I wish you'd never heard of it!"

The angry conversation ceased. George spoke up. "Sounds like trouble."

Nancy agreed. "And like a pair of mysteries," she added with a smile.

Presently she looked at her wristwatch. The twenty minutes were up, so she suggested that the girls go back to the restaurant. As they neared the log where the couple had been seated, they saw that the girl and her male companion were gone.

Bess sighed. "Oh, I just hope they fixed everything up."

George said, "They'd better solve those mysteries before they get married. A lawsuit and some problem over an iron bird don't sound good to me!"

The dinner was delicious. Bess could not resist topping hers off with pecan pie. "That's a real Southern dessert and I am now in Maryland."

"Don't forget, dear cousin," George told her, "that during the Civil War Maryland was on the Northern side."

"I don't care," said Bess. "This pie is marvelous."

Just as she finished, Bess clapped a hand to her ear. "My earring! It's gone again!" Bess declared she knew exactly where it had fallen off. "When I was coming back across that old bridge I tripped on one of the broken planks. Oh, I hope my earring didn't fall into the water!"

Nancy suggested that they take a look, so after paying their bill, the three girls hurried back to the bridge. Nancy peered beneath the railing at one side.

"There it is!" She pointed. "On the muddy bank." She lay down on the floor of the bridge, her head and shoulders over the side. Then she wriggled forward and reached her arm toward the earring. She could not quite touch it.

"Hold my feet, George, so I can stretch farther," Nancy directed.

"All right."

Bess, meanwhile, stood on the edge of the slippery embankment, watching nervously. Suddenly she heard running footsteps and looked up. Hurrying toward the bridge was the red-haired girl they had seen earlier.

"Wait!" Bess called to her, afraid the rickety structure would not hold the trio's combined weight.

But the girl paid no attention. She dashed onto the bridge and ran across just as Nancy managed to grab the earring. At that moment the planking pulled away from the embankment. Thrown off balance, the three on the bridge toppled over the side!

CHAPTER II

The Phantom Launch

BESS screamed as the three girls landed on the muddy slope below the bridge. Nancy and George caught hold of a low shrub, but the red-haired girl rolled toward the water. Quickly Nancy reached out and caught her arm.

"Are you all right?" Bess called down as the girls struggled to their feet.

Nancy tried to smile. "I'm sure we look like wrecks, but at least we're in one piece."

The strange young woman did not speak until they reached the garden of the White Mill restaurant. Then she said, "I should have realized that bridge wasn't safe. I guess my added weight made it give way. Please forgive me."

"Don't worry," Bess told her, then added ruefully, "Nancy, I shouldn't have let you rescue my earring. Thanks a million."

George declared that if the accident were anyone's fault, it was that of the restaurant owners.

"I'll report it," said Nancy. Turning to the stranger, whose clothes were muddy and her face tear-stained, Nancy asked if there was anything the girls could do for her.

"Thank you, no," came the answer.

Bess, curious about the girl's problem with her fiancé, tried to draw her out. Smiling, Bess said, "Maybe my friend Nancy Drew here can help you in a special way. She's a detective."

The young woman looked startled, but she revealed nothing about herself and did not offer to give her name. Again she said, "Thank you, no," but suddenly burst out, "Oh, I've made such a mess of my life! Well, good-by. You were wonderful to save me from going into the water, Nancy." With that, she hurried off through the garden and disappeared around the front of the restaurant.

Mystified, Nancy and her friends walked toward the building. They heard a car start up and assumed the young woman was driving it.

Bess began to fume. "Here we come upon a real romantic mystery, and now we'll never know the answer."

George looked at her cousin severely. "I'm surprised at you. That girl's affairs are her own business. Why should she confide in us?"

Her cousin sighed, but said no more on the subject. Nancy went directly to the restaurant manager and told him about the bridge. The man was apologetic, explaining that he had meant to close it until repairs could be made. "I've been so busy that I'm afraid it slipped my mind. I'll pay for the damages," he added quickly.

Nancy and George replied that this would not be necessary. They took their bags from the car and went to the powder room of the inn to wash and put on fresh dresses.

When they came outside again, Nancy and her friends climbed into the convertible and set off for Misty Lake. It was dusk when they arrived in the small, old-fashioned town. There was one main street with a few other roads branching off from it.

"Dad told me to find out if some bottled gas had been delivered to the Baker cottage," Nancy remarked.

She drove along slowly and finally spotted a darkened building marked: STERN BROTHERS FUEL COMPANY. There was a light in a room at the rear. "Maybe the watchman's in there," said Nancy, and pulled into the driveway.

The girls hopped out, and Nancy knocked on the back door. After a few minutes it was opened by an elderly man who stared at them in surprise.

"Place is closed," he said tersely.

"I know," said Nancy. "I just wanted to ask you a question. Have you delivered gas to the Baker cottage recently?"

"Of course not," he said. "The cottage is locked up for the winter."

Nancy explained that someone had rented it for a couple of weeks and she had come to open it up. "We'll certainly need gas," she said. "Would it be possible for someone to take a tank down there this evening?"

"Nope," he answered shortly. "There's probably some firewood out back of the cottage. Listen! I wouldn't deliver gas down there at night if it was the last thing I did. If you knew what I know, you'd stay away from that place too."

Bess gave a little cry of dismay. "What's the matter with it?" she asked fearfully.

"I ain't saying. You ask Henry Winch," the man replied.

Nancy cajoled him for several minutes, but he stood firm in his refusal to say more. Nancy returned to the car and backed into the street.

At once Bess spoke up. "Nancy, I don't want to go near the cottage tonight, either. Not for a million dollars!"

George grinned. "Never fear. We brave ones will protect you."

Nancy diverted Bess's attention by pointing out a neat white frame house with a sign: GUESTS. "That looks nice," she said. "It must be the guest place Dad mentioned."

Nancy pulled up and the three girls went in to

inquire about accommodations. The house was owned by a Mrs. Hosking. She was very friendly and her home was immaculate.

Mrs. Hosking said, "Yes, I have a large front room on the second floor with three beds. Tell me, are you girls on a trip?"

"Well, sort of," Nancy replied. "We have the key for the person who has rented the Baker cottage. Then we'd like to find Mr. Winch."

Mrs. Hosking shuddered. "I can tell you where Henry is—visiting his brother in Ridgeton, our county seat. But listen, girls, don't you go down to that cottage—especially at night. Why, just two days ago Henry came dashing in here white as a ghost. Now, he's not a man who scares easy. He declared he'd seen the lost launch."

"What is that? And why should it scare him?" Nancy asked.

Mrs. Hosking explained that around the turn of the century there had been a large picnic grove at the far end of the lake. An excursion launch had carried parties up to the picnic grounds.

"One night the launch sprang a leak and went down quickly. Everyone on board was trapped and lost."

"How shocking!" Bess murmured.

"After that," Mrs. Hosking went on, "the picnic spot became unpopular and soon no one went there any more."

"But what does this have to do with now?"
George asked.

Mrs. Hosking's voice dropped to a whisper.
"Many people have been saying that recently the
ill-fated launch and its passengers have been seen
at night through the mist near the picnic grove."

Bess hunched her shoulders. "That sounds absolutely spooky."

"It is," Mrs. Hosking said. "And more than
spooky. I've known Henry Winch all my life. If
he says he saw that old launch, then I know he did.
I beg you girls to stay away."

Nancy smiled. "We appreciate your warning,"
she said. "Don't worry, Mrs. Hosking. We'll be
back. Please tell me how to get to the Baker cottage."

Reluctantly, Mrs. Hosking gave directions. The
girls started off down the main street where they
would turn into a dirt lane that led down to the
lake. On the way, Bess spotted a small grocery
store that was open and begged Nancy to stop so
that she could pick up a few items. "I know we'll
all be starving before we get to bed. Remember,
we had a very early dinner."

Grinning, Nancy complied. When Bess returned from the shop, she was carrying a large bag
which she said contained milk, cocoa, cookies, and
ham sandwiches. Nancy and George wanted to
tease her, but refrained. It was just possible that

Bess was right and they *would* all be hungry by
bedtime.

By this time it was dark. Nancy drove slowly so
that she would not miss the dirt lane. She turned
left onto it and they rode nearly a mile before
coming to the bluff which rimmed the large oval
lake. All the houses seemed to be closed up for the
season. The girls could not see a light.

The lane branched left and right along the
edge of the bluff. Mrs. Hosking had told Nancy
to take the left-hand fork, which wound down
among trees to a row of cottages. After passing two
of them, they came to Henry Winch's dock and
small store. As they rode on, Bess kept her eyes
nervously on the water, wondering if they would
see the strange apparition of the picnic launch,
but nothing appeared. They drove by two more
cottages, and when they came to the third, Nancy
turned off the motor.

"This is it," she said.

From the roadway, a narrow footpath led among
evergreen and birch trees to the Baker cottage,
near one end of the lake. The girls took out flashlights and started down the path. They had not
gone far when they were startled to hear footsteps
almost directly behind them. Recalling Mrs. Hosking's warning, they turned and shone their lights
on the oncoming figure.

"That mysterious girl again!" Nancy gasped

Nancy gave a gasp of surprise. "That mysterious girl again!"

It was indeed the young woman from the White Mill restaurant!

She was wearing a light raincoat and a head scarf, out of which peeked curly red hair. A thought flashed through Nancy's mind. Could this be Cecily Curtis?

The stranger stared in astonishment. She stood for a moment without saying anything, then suddenly turned and ran up the path.

"Cecily! Are you Cecily?" Nancy cried out.

The fleeing figure paused and whirled about. A look of terror crossed her face as she cried out:

"You can't stop me from getting the babies!"

The next moment she had rushed off and vanished from sight.

CHAPTER III

Mistaken Identity

As the distraught girl vanished into the darkness, Nancy, Bess, and George stood still. They were completely puzzled. Was Cecily Curtis the red-haired young woman they had seen at the White Mill restaurant?

"But why would she run away from us?" Bess asked.

"And what did she mean about the babies?" George added.

Nancy reminded the cousins that they were all assuming the young woman was Cecily Curtis. "We ought to know soon, one way or the other. It's getting late."

When the girls reached the cottage on the lake front they looked up to the opposite end of the lake, a scant half mile away. A heavy mist shrouded it. Nancy guessed there might be hot springs in that area, which would account for the unusually heavy vapor. The moon was rising and revealed several cottages in the distance to their right.

Suddenly Bess said, "Look up on the bluff about halfway to the far end of the lake! There's a big house with a light in the second floor. Somebody's staying there!"

"Maybe," said George, "it's an all-year home."

As Nancy unlocked the door of the Baker cottage, Bess remarked, "It *is* eerie around this place. I'll be glad to get back to town."

George said sternly, "Now don't be imagining things."

"Well, if I do," Bess retorted, "I'm in good company. Mrs. Hosking advised us not to come here and Henry Winch, who isn't a 'fraidy cat, got enough of a scare to make him leave the lake."

Nancy laughed. "At least the Baker cottage is okay. No ghosts here!"

She beamed her flashlight about the interior. The living-dining room stretched across the front of the house and was comfortably furnished. Books and magazines on low tables and a huge fireplace gave the room a homelike atmosphere. George spotted a kerosene lamp, and with matches from the mantelshelf, lighted it.

"How cozy!" Bess exclaimed. "I'll bet it's wonderful in the summer with swimming and boating and everything. But why in the world would anybody want to come here alone this time of the year?"

"Fall is beautiful," George answered. "Maybe some people just like to look at the fall foliage."

The cottage was in perfect order, but the beds were not made and there was no food. Nancy built a fire in a wood stove in the kitchen and Bess prepared cocoa. George soon had a fire roaring in the fireplace and before long the chill of the cabin was gone. As the girls waited for Cecily, they talked about their experiences and conceded the day had been full of surprises.

Finally Nancy looked at her watch. "Do you realize it is ten o'clock and Cecily hasn't come yet?"

"What'll we do?" Bess asked. "We can't sit up all night."

Nancy suddenly proposed, "Why don't we sleep here? Cecily may not arrive until very late."

This plan was agreed upon, although reluctantly on Bess's part. George offered to drive back to town and tell Mrs. Hosking of the girls' change in plans.

"In the meantime, I'll make up some beds," Bess offered.

"And if you don't mind," said Nancy, "I'd like to do a little investigating outdoors."

Bess warned her to be careful. Nancy said she would not go far. "Just down to Henry Winch's dock."

She rode that far with George, then got out of the car and went down a path to the dock. To one side of it was a good-sized boathouse, and with moonlight streaming into the windows, Nancy could see motorboats, rowboats, and canoes. On the other side of the dock was the confectionery store with Mr. Winch's living quarters behind it. From the end of the dock, Nancy had a clear view of the whole lake—cottages, the large house on the bluff, and the mist-shrouded end of the lake.

The young sleuth smiled to herself. "I wish that phantom boat *would* appear! I'd like to know what it looks like."

But there was no sign of any ghostly vessel, and finally Nancy walked back to the cottage along a path near the lake front. She heard a car coming and wondered whether it was George returning, or Cecily Curtis arriving. She hurried up to the road to find out.

The car proved to be her own and in a moment George alighted. She had brought a few supplies which Mrs. Hosking had given her for the girls' breakfast.

"I insisted upon paying her for the food," said George, "and also a fair amount for holding our room."

"I'm glad you did that," said Nancy.

"We'd better take our bags," said George. They took them from the trunk, locked the car, then the two girls started in silence down the wooded path. They were about halfway to the cottage when suddenly they heard soft rustling in the bushes at the top of the slope above. The next moment something black shot past them!

The girls jumped, wondering what the object was.

"Some animal, I think," said Nancy. "We must have scared it."

The words were hardly out of her mouth when a high, clear voice called, "Satin, come back here!"

Nancy and George turned. Someone was starting down the path. It must be Cecily!

The two girls set down their bags and started forward to greet her. Nancy called out "Hello," as she beamed her flashlight up the hill.

The girl from the White Mill restaurant again! But this time she was not wearing the raincoat and scarf. She had on the same outfit they had seen at the restaurant, and was lugging two suitcases.

"Oh, hello!" she said pleasantly. "Well, this is a nice surprise! Are you vacationing here?"

Nancy and George were confounded. Hadn't the newcomer recognized them? And why had she changed her clothes again?

"Are you Cecily Curtis?" Nancy asked as the girls hastened to help her.

"Yes, I am. But how did you know?"

Nancy, though bewildered, decided to ask no

questions, but she did notice the girl was not yet wearing a wedding ring. She introduced herself and George. "Mr. Winch is out of town, so we came here with the key to open the cottage for you."

"How wonderful!" Cecily said.

"What is Satin?" George asked, taking one of the bags.

"My big black cat. I dropped his carrying case and it opened. He zipped out of it like lightning."

Nancy chuckled. "He flew right past George and me."

Cecily stopped short. "I just recognized you both! It was so dark and I was so startled I didn't realize I'd met you at the White Mill. Imagine! Especially after you rescued me, Nancy! But there were three of you. What happened to the other girl?"

"Bess Marvin is in the cottage making up beds." Nancy smiled. "Now that you are here, though, we'll go back to town for rooms."

"Oh, I'd be delighted to have you stay," Cecily declared. "Really, I would! To tell the truth, I'm pretty lonesome."

"We'll accept with pleasure!" said Nancy.

By this time the three had entered the cottage. At once Bess exclaimed, "I'm so glad you got here, Cecily! We were terribly worried. Why didn't you stay the first time you came?"

Cecily looked at her blankly. "The first time? I haven't been here before."

It was Bess's turn to look perplexed. "You mean you weren't up in the woods on your way here a few hours ago?"

Cecily shook her head. "If you thought you saw me, I must have a double in the vicinity." She changed the subject. "I had an awful time getting to this cottage. A bus brought me to Misty Lake village from Baltimore, and I tried to get a taxi to bring me here. Nobody wanted to, but finally one man agreed to drive me as far as the end of the lane. I had to lug these bags and my cat all the rest of the way."

"You poor thing!" Bess said sympathetically.

Nancy, Bess, and George had agreed tacitly not to mention having overheard Cecily and her fiancé talking. If she felt like telling them, however, they would be interested listeners!

Nancy said, "Don't you think we'd better find Satin?"

Cecily nodded, and the four took flashlights and went outside. Nancy gave the key to Cecily, who locked the cottage door. The girls began the search. Cecily kept calling the cat by name, but he did not come.

"Oh, dear!" Cecily sighed. "Satin is such a comfort to me. I shall just die if he is gone."

Without being sure where to look next, the girls

finally turned right. They passed the neighboring cottages, then Henry Winch's dock and continued along the lake front toward the stone house, atop the bluff. Cecily kept calling softly to her pet. Finally George spotted two glowing eyes peering from behind a tree and whispered to Cecily, "I'll bet that's Satin!"

"Here kitty, kitty, kitty!" Cecily said quietly. "Come here, Satin!"

Reluctantly, the big black cat came toward her. She scooped him up in her arms and patted him affectionately.

Through the stillness of the woods, Nancy detected a strange sound. "Listen!" she said quickly.

They all stood motionless. Amid the chirps of myriad crickets and the hoots of an owl, the girls could hear a steady humming noise. It was not far from them. What could it be?

CHAPTER IV

The Wailing Cry

THE girls listened intently as the strange humming noise continued. It was muffled.

"That must be a machine," Nancy remarked. "But what kind and where is it?"

"It's probably just a pump," George said practically.

Bess looked doubtful. "I thought pumps made a thumping noise."

"Let's try to find the thing," Nancy suggested. "It sounds close."

The girls searched the wooded bluff nearby, and a short distance along the shore on either side, but found no explanation for the noise. Puzzled, they returned to the beach.

Nancy looked up at the big stone house. The light was still on. Could the machine be in there? Was the sound being carried by the wind? As the thought crossed her mind, she suddenly realized that a man stood silhouetted in a doorway.

"Someone's up there," Nancy told the others. "He must have seen our flashlights."

George giggled. "I suppose he thinks we're burglars!"

Cecily did not comment, but stared at the house as if fascinated. Nancy, seeing her frown, remembered her father's remark that Cecily had an interesting story. What was it? And did the big stone house have something to do with the girl's reason for coming to the lake?

"Let's go!" Bess urged.

"Good idea," Cecily agreed. "I wonder—" She stopped speaking and turned away.

The other girls did not ask for any explanation, but all of them felt that Cecily, though friendly enough, was rather secretive. Nancy chided herself, however, that there was no reason why Cecily should immediately start telling them her personal problems.

The man went inside the house again and in a few moments the humming noise stopped. The girls wondered if he had turned off whatever machine had been causing the sound. Within minutes the big stone house was in darkness and Nancy assumed that whoever lived there had gone to bed.

The girls picked their way carefully back to the cottage, unlocked it, and went inside. Bess, overcome by curiosity, asked Cecily if she had come to the lake for a late vacation.

"Why—yes," Cecily answered noncommittally. She yawned. "If you don't mind, I think I'll go to bed. I've had a tiring day."

The others agreed that this was true indeed. The day had not only been tiring for her, but apparently very worrisome. It was arranged that Cecily and Nancy would sleep in one of the two bedrooms, and George and Bess in the other. The cat, Satin, was made comfortable on a small pillow from one of Cecily's bags. The soft, furry animal, cuddled by the fireplace, began to purr, and was soon asleep.

The girls had a snack and then went to bed. Nancy dropped off to sleep almost immediately, but was rudely awakened by the shrill cry of a woman outside. She and Cecily sat upright at the same moment, then jumped out of bed and rushed into the living room. As the screaming continued, Bess and George also appeared and all four girls ran from the cottage.

"Who is it? Where is she?" Bess asked, glancing fearfully around in the darkness.

The screaming seemed to be coming from the woods just beyond the cottage. The girls could see nothing, so Nancy rushed back inside for her flashlight and beamed it at the trees.

Suddenly there was a rustle of leaves and a huge

bird left its perch on the branches of an oak. It flew directly in front of the girls, then soared out over the lake.

Nancy began to laugh. "We got fooled that time, all right. That bird is a loon. I just remembered that their call can be easily mistaken for a woman's scream."

"Well, for Pete's sake!" said George in disgust. "All kinds of things have awakened me in my life but never a crazy old bird!"

As the girls re-entered the cottage, the black cat lazily rose, arched his back, then gave a huge yawn. Bess giggled. "Satin, you're the only creature here who knows the difference between a birdcall and a screaming woman!"

Again Satin settled down, the house was locked, and the girls went to bed. Nancy did not go to sleep at once and she noticed that Cecily seemed restless, too. The young sleuth thought it best not to speak to her new acquaintance, however, and finally dropped off to sleep.

Presently Nancy was awakened once more, this time by a loud miaowing. She wondered what was bothering the cat, and looked over to see if Cecily were awake. She noticed that the red-haired girl was not in her bed.

At first Nancy assumed that she had gone out to quiet Satin, but as the animal persisted in its miaowing, Nancy finally got up. To her amazement,

Cecily was not in the cottage. The cat was wailing and scratching at the front door.

Nancy thought, "Perhaps Cecily couldn't sleep, and went for a walk." Thinking she might comfort the girl, Nancy quietly went outside but left Satin in the cottage.

The moon had now risen bright and clear, but its light did not reveal Cecily. A bit alarmed, Nancy called the girl's name softly. There was no answer.

"Oh, dear, I hope she didn't run away!" Nancy said to herself. "Maybe my being here with Bess and George disturbed her. But she did seem sincere in wanting us to stay."

On a hunch Nancy went back into the cottage. Cecily's suitcases were there, and also her pajamas, neatly folded on a chair. Apparently she had changed into outdoor clothes! Quickly Nancy put on slacks and a sweater. She took her flashlight and once more hurried outside. For a moment she was tempted to awaken Bess and George but did not want to waste precious time. She paused for a few seconds, trying to figure which direction Cecily might have followed.

"Toward the road to town?" Nancy asked herself.

She discarded this idea because the girl had not taken her luggage along. "And I don't see her along the lake front."

Suddenly the young sleuth recalled how fascinated Cecily had been by the large stone house
near which they had heard the strange humming
sound.

"Maybe Cecily went back there out of curiosity.
Anyway, that's where I'm going to look."

There was the semblance of a path through the
woods, a short distance above the water, leading
toward the foot of the bluff. Nancy followed this,
keeping her eyes open for the missing girl and
calling her name. She did not see Cecily, nor was
there any reply.

Nancy went on and on and in a short time the
path curved away from the lake and went directly
up the steep embankment. The thick woods shut
out the brilliant moonlight and Nancy turned on
her flashlight. Again she paused, undecided
whether to go on. The path led up to the big
house, and if this were Cecily's goal, perhaps she
had taken it.

"I'll try it," Nancy determined.

She was about halfway up the slope when suddenly her heart gave a thump and she nearly
stopped breathing. Off to one side of the path, the
missing girl lay in a crumpled heap!

"Oh, Cecily!" Nancy exclaimed as she rushed
over to the still figure.

She felt Cecily's pulse and found that she was
alive. The unconscious girl had a large swelling on

her temple. Had she fallen and hit her head? Or, worse, had she been struck by some unknown assailant?

Cautiously Nancy looked all around and listened. At the head of the steep path she noticed a short, thick log, blocking the exit to the top of the bluff. But there was no sign of life.

"I must revive Cecily," Nancy thought. She hastened down to the lake where she wet a clean handkerchief, then hurried back. As she was bathing the injured girl's face, she heard a twig crack on the bluff above her.

Nancy looked up quickly. To her horror, the heavy log was rolling at breakneck speed down the path directly toward them!

CHAPTER V.

The Iron Bird

THERE was not a second to lose. Nancy seized the unconscious girl and rolled off the path with her. The log sped past, grazing Nancy's shoulder. Moments later, she heard it thud to the beach below and then splash into the water.

As Nancy breathed a sigh of relief, her companion stirred and opened her eyes. "Cecily, are you all right?" Nancy asked anxiously.

For a moment the girl looked bewildered, then she said, "Yes," and sat up.

"I'm certainly thankful for that!" Nancy exclaimed.

The young detective rubbed her bruised shoulder and looked thoughtfully up the path. She wondered why the log had started rolling and remembered the twig she had heard crack. Had someone deliberately shoved the log down on them? No one was in sight and right now there was no chance of her finding out the answer to her question.

"Oh, Nancy! You've saved me twice!" Cecily said weakly. "Pl-please help me back to the cottage, and I'll tell you why I came here."

The injured girl found it difficult to walk, but with Nancy's arm firmly supporting her, they slowly made their way through the woods. Dawn was breaking when the two girls reached the cottage.

In the meantime, Bess and George had been awakened by the miaowing cat and had become frantic over the missing girls. "What on earth happened?" Bess demanded. "You both look awful!"

The cousins were horrified upon hearing that Cecily had been knocked unconscious.

"Of course I'm not sure that it was a person who did it," Cecily said quickly. "I—I just remember hearing a noise and—" Her voice trailed off.

Bess, realizing how exhausted the girl was, advised her not to talk any further. "You and Nancy sleep. When you wake up, I'll have breakfast all ready."

Everyone agreed and in minutes the foursome were sound asleep. It was after nine o'clock when the girls sat down to the excellent meal Bess had prepared. Cecily said she felt fine, regardless of the bump on her head.

After they had eaten, she smiled and said, "You all have been wonderful to me. I know I can trust you completely, so I'm going to tell you two big secrets of mine. The first one concerns an iron bird."

Nancy, Bess, and George leaned forward eagerly. Cecily explained that her story dated back to the Civil War. Her father's family had been wealthy at that time, and was reputed to have hidden a fortune just before hostilities started.

"I don't know much about my great-great-grandfather, except that he was a Northerner and his first name was William. He and his wife were drowned trying to escape from New Orleans at the outbreak of the war. Their three-year-old daughter, Amelia, was rescued and placed in an orphanage. An official there said the child had remembered only her first name and the fact that she used to live 'in a big pudding stone house on a lake!'

"Also, Amelia was wearing on a chain around her neck half of a gold locket with a thin paper rolled under the picture rim. The paper had a message—'*Will, I hid your half of fortune. Directions in the iron bird. Your brother Simon.*'"

Cecily went on to say that as Amelia grew older, she tried without success to trace her background, as well as the fortune. "Of course lots of records in those days had been lost or destroyed. Later,

Amelia married Robert Curtis. Their grandson was my father."

Cecily looked wistful. "I can just barely remember Daddy telling Mother the story which Amelia had learned from the orphanage official. He had tried to find the fortune, too, but no luck!" Cecily explained that her own parents had died when she was seven. From then on, she had been under the guardianship of an elderly cousin of her mother's. Upon the cousin's death several years ago, Cecily had been left on her own.

"At least," she said, "I still had my great-grandmother's half of the locket and made up my mind to find the fortune myself, if possible."

"And you came here to search for the iron bird?" asked Nancy, greatly intrigued.

"Yes. I studied loads of maps, trying to dig up some clue. Finally I came upon a really old map, and found the name Pudding Stone Lake. I went on hunting, and learned that Misty Lake here is the very same place. The name was changed."

"How fascinating!" Bess said.

George added, "And you believe the iron bird may be connected with the stone house Amelia remembered? And that they're both in this vicinity?"

Cecily nodded. "I have a strong hunch they are. The house on the bluff is all of stone, and looks pretty old. So last night I decided to go out by myself and get a good close-up view of the place." She smiled ruefully. "But I didn't get very far."

Cecily arose and went to her suitcase. From it she brought out the half of a small heart-shaped locket, and Simon's note.

Nancy's mind was racing. She mentioned the other red-haired girl and asked Cecily if she had a relative who resembled her closely. "Maybe that girl we saw is hiding here because she's searching for the same thing you are!"

"I don't know anyone who looks like me," Cecily replied. "I have no close relatives, but I may have distant cousins whom I don't even know."

Suddenly Cecily changed the subject. "Now that I'm here and all these strange things are happening, I admit I'm afraid to be alone. Would it be possible for you girls to stay here and help me solve the mystery?"

The three grinned and Nancy said, "I'd love to. How about you, Bess and George?"

"I'm too intrigued to leave now," Bess answered, and George said, "I think, Cecily, that you and Nancy need a strong, athletic person around to help keep guard. Maybe I can fill the bill!"

"Wonderful!" said Cecily. "And now I'd like to tell you my other secret."

She explained that she was engaged to a young man named Niko Van Dyke. "He's a pop singer and leads his own combo which is called the Flying Dutchmen."

"Oh, I love their music," said Bess, exchanging glances with Nancy and George. Now they understood why the young man who had been with Cecily had seemed familiar. They had seen Niko's picture in newspapers and magazines.

Cecily went on, "Niko is just starting to become famous, mostly because of his latest record. Polls show it to be a hit number, but the mystery is that his royalty payments don't match its popularity. Niko is suing the record company for withholding his rightful share of profit."

"Well, I should think he would," George said indignantly.

Cecily said that the company denied any dishonesty. "I feel that Niko and I shouldn't get married while the lawsuit is pending. He has little money, what with paying off loans he got for his college education and his music instruction. I have a job in New Orleans, but of course when I marry Niko, I'll want to travel with him, and at present we just can't afford it."

"That's a shame!" Bess remarked.

Cecily nodded. "Perhaps it's foolish of me to be too hopeful, but I thought if I could only find that treasure, then everything would be fine and Niko and I could get married."

"Where is he now?" Nancy asked.

"In Baltimore. He asked me to meet him at the White Mill restaurant." Cecily's eyes filled with tears. "Then he begged me to go with him to Baltimore and get married. When I wouldn't, he became angry and blamed everything on the iron bird. I was dreadfully upset. I'd like to try to reach him on the phone. Will you drive me to town, please?"

"Yes, indeed," Nancy replied. "If we're going to stay here, we'll need food supplies and fuel. Also, I'll have to call Dad and let him know where we are."

After tidying the cottage, the girls set off. When they reached the lane that led to the village, Nancy stopped. "What say we take a few minutes and drive up to the stone house?"

The others were eager to go so she drove straight along the top of the bluff. As they neared their destination, Cecily suddenly cried out, "Look! That sign ahead!"

CHAPTER VI

The Phantom Ship

ALL the girls stared excitedly at the sign. It said:

PUDDING STONE LODGE
PRIVATE

"Pudding Stone!" Nancy exclaimed. "Perhaps it's called that after the lake's original name—which would mean that it dates back many years."

"Oh, let's talk to the owner!" Cecily urged.

The girls peered ahead eagerly as Nancy drove on. In a few moments they came to a large, open garage in which two trucks were parked. On the side of each was painted:

DRISCOLL BROTHERS
PLANT MAINTENANCE

About an eighth of a mile farther on they came to the bluff house. It was built of stones of various shapes and sizes.

"That must be why it's called Pudding Stone Lodge," George said.

"It's certainly old-looking." Bess pointed to the roof. It was irregular in design, with sloping sides broken by peaks and turrets.

Cecily was excited and wanted to rush up to the door at once. Nancy held her back, reminding her that she had been injured on the grounds of the lodge only the evening before.

"I'll go." Nancy got out of the car and went up to the front door. Her ring was answered by a short, burly man with heavy black hair.

"Mr. Driscoll?" Nancy asked pleasantly. "Do you own this house?"

"No. I rent it. What's that to you?"

"It's so attractive, we girls thought we would like to look around the grounds a little. Do you mind?"

"Yes, I do," the man said in a surly tone. "Get out of here and don't return!"

Nancy was taken aback. She did not argue and turned away, deciding that they had better not tarry. What was the reason for the man's belligerence? "Very odd," she mused, "to act like that. Could he possibly be responsible for Cecily's injury or know about it?"

As she drove off, Nancy explained to the girls what the man had said and her suspicions. Cecily looked worried. "Oh, dear! How am I ever going

"Get out of here and don't return!"

to hunt there for the iron bird if we're not to be allowed on the property? It might even be in the house."

George grinned. "Nancy will think of a way, I promise you that!"

The others laughed and then became quiet until they reached town. Here the girls separated. George offered to go and order bottled gas from the fuel company. Cecily went to telephone Niko. Nancy and Bess headed toward the general store to shop for supplies.

The proprietor, Mr. Joplin, was an inquisitive person. "You're newcomers around here," he said.

"Yes, we are," Nancy answered. She introduced herself and Bess. Noticing two other men in the store, she felt it wiser not to give any more details.

Bess, however, was not so cautious. She blurted out that the four girls were staying in the Baker cottage, and that it certainly was a scary place. At this remark one of the two men, tall and pale with hard eyes, stared intently at the girls.

The shopkeeper chuckled. "You mean you've been scared by the loons?"

"Yes, and—" Nancy squeezed Bess's arm so she would say no more.

Nancy was about to begin her shopping when the heavy-set customer came over to the girls.

"Are you Carson Drew's daughter Nancy?" he asked.

When Nancy nodded, he added, "Sure pleased to meet such a famous young detective. I'm Henry Winch. I mailed the cottage key to your father so I suppose he sent you here with it."

"That's right." Just then the young sleuth noticed the tall, thin man gazing at her with narrowed eyes. He turned abruptly and left the shop.

"Who was that man?" Nancy asked.

Both the proprietor and Henry Winch said they did not know. It was the first time he had been in the store.

The girls asked Mr. Winch about the phantom launch. He proved to be talkative, and vividly described the ghostly craft.

"The old boat drifts along in the mist," Winch went on, "and then when it reaches the spot where it's supposed to have gone down, it vanishes." The caretaker shuddered. "Started a couple o' weeks ago. Summer folks began leavin' earlier than usual. If they're scared to come back next season I'll lose business. I'm thinkin' of sellin' out and goin' back to my brother's—to stay."

Nancy and Bess, although sympathetic, did not comment. They quickly purchased the items they needed, then said good-by and left.

They met George and Cecily at the car. George announced the bottled gas would be delivered soon. Also, she had stopped at Mrs. Hosking's to inquire about Pudding Stone Lodge. She learned that it belonged to the Kenneth Wayne family of Baltimore, who had rented the house early in the summer to two brothers named Driscoll.

"Oh, I must telephone the Waynes right away!" said Cecily. She told the others she had not been able to get hold of Niko either at his hotel or the theater where he was playing. "I did leave word I was at the cottage with friends," she said, and sighed. "Oh, I just hope he isn't too upset!"

Cecily hurried off to telephone the Waynes, and Nancy went to call her father. She learned that he would be away on a business trip for a couple of weeks and wished her luck in the mysteries.

"But don't take unnecessary chances," Mr. Drew cautioned.

"I'll do my best not to," Nancy replied. "Goodby, Dad, and lots of luck to you too."

Cecily reported that she had been unable to get an answer to her phone call. The girls climbed into Nancy's convertible and headed back to the cottage. As they reached the end of the lane a man suddenly stepped into the road, directly in their path. He was the tall, thin man from the general store!

He held up his hand and ordered, "Stop!"

Nancy had no choice but to obey. To the girls' surprise, the thin man smiled at them and came up to the car. "Don't be worried," he said. "I'm Karl Driscoll. I heard my brother Vince ordered you off our property and I came to apologize. There's no reason why you girls shouldn't look around the grounds. You're welcome any time."

He smirked and went on, "I have a hunch you're not just sightseers. You looking for something?"

Nancy would have preferred that the girls say nothing, but Cecily spoke up eagerly. "Yes, I'm looking for an iron bird. I have no idea what it looks like, and I'm not sure whether the lodge is the place for me to search. My ancestors once lived in a similar house, though, and I'm curious to find out if this is the one."

Karl Driscoll showed great interest. "An iron bird, eh? Sounds unusual," he said. "I wish I could help you, but I haven't seen any such bird around since we rented the place. I'll keep a lookout, though."

He said he must be leaving and walked off toward Pudding Stone Lodge. Nancy had a sudden hunch that he would search for the iron bird himself—that he probably suspected there was more to the whole story than Cecily had revealed.

"What do you make of all that?" George asked with suspicion in her tone. "One brother is surly and the other goes out of his way to apologize."

"It is strange," Nancy admitted. "I think we should take advantage of Karl Driscoll's offer and inspect the grounds very soon."

Cecily was eager to do so and it was decided that they would go directly after luncheon. Back at the cottage, the girls were delighted to find that bottled gas had been delivered.

"Oh boy, hot water!" Bess exclaimed. "Me for a relaxing bath."

"Not now," George said. "Sleuthing comes first."

The girls had a quick lunch and directly afterward put on hiking clothes and shoes and started up the lake path to Pudding Stone Lodge. From boundary markers they discovered that the property was very large. Their search went on all afternoon, both in the vicinity of the stone house itself and over the grounds. There was no sign of an iron bird.

Finally Bess suggested they give up. "I'm so tired I could break into pieces," she said. "Let's go back to the cottage."

Though disappointed, the others agreed. They luxuriated in hot baths, rested for a little while, and then had supper. Afterward, Cecily proposed that they go to town. "I'd like to try telephoning Niko and the Waynes again."

At seven o'clock they set off for the village. All the stores were closed with the exception of Eddie's Soda Shop.

As Cecily went into a phone booth, the other girls engaged Eddie in conversation. They learned he was a newcomer in town but was doing very well.

"People around here must like ice cream," Bess remarked.

"They sure do. In fact, people come from miles away to get my ice cream. It's good as homemade."

"In that case, I can't resist a double helping," Bess said with a giggle.

"What kind?"

"Vanilla," Bess replied with a twinkle. "With hot fudge sauce."

"Coming right up," said Eddie.

Nancy and George said they would take the same. As they were being served, Cecily came from the booth and sat down at the table.

Eddie stared at her. "I'm glad you came in," he said. "The record you ordered is here." He grinned. "You owe me a dollar."

Cecily in turn stared at him in amazement. "I've never been in your shop before," she said. "This is the second time I've been mistaken for another girl. I'd certainly like to meet her!"

Eddie looked bewildered. "Well, if you say so, it must be true." He shook his head. "But you two girls sure look alike."

"Where does the girl live?" Nancy asked.

Eddie shrugged. "She didn't say. Just told me she'd be back. Say, the record's nifty—Niko Van Dyke's latest."

His listeners were astounded. Cecily cried out, "Niko's record! Why, he—I—" She did not finish the sentence.

The girls did not explain to Eddie, but Nancy asked if he would mind playing the record. "And if you have another, I'll buy it."

"I have plenty now. They sell like hot cakes. I can't keep 'em on hand long." He went into a back room.

Cecily was blinking furiously, on the verge of tears. She explained to the girls that she had failed again to reach the Waynes or Niko. "I'm so worried," she said. "He may be really angry. I wish I could see him!"

Nancy said soothingly, "I am sure you will soon."

Eddie came back with a record and played it for them. The girls listened intently to the Flying Dutchmen's number and at the end voted it an excellent piece.

"It's Niko's best," said Eddie. "He must be making a pile of money!"

A pained expression came over Cecily's face and George quickly suggested she have some ice cream. "Thanks, but I'm—I'm not hungry," said the red-haired girl.

When the others had finished eating, Nancy picked up the record and they left. George, who was ahead of the others, stopped to look in a shop next door. It was called the Gift Emporium. She called her friends' attention to the display window. In it, hanging as a wall plaque, was an ornamental iron bird.

"This gives me an idea," said George. "Let's ask if there's an ironmonger around here. He might still have some information in old files of an iron bird having been made long ago for Pudding Stone Lodge."

Cecily brightened at once. "That's a great idea, George," she said. "We can start inquiring tomorrow."

After this, Cecily acted more like her animated self and conversation was lively and cheerful on the way home.

As they were about to unlock the door to the cottage, Bess, who was facing the lake, gave a scream. "Listen! Look!"

The others turned in her direction. They could hear a ship's bell ringing! Up at the misty end of the lake, the girls were startled to see an old-time excursion launch, brightly lighted. It moved slowly, as if against a buffeting wind.

Passengers, dressed in clothes of the early 1900's, walked about freely. They were talking and laughing.

"The phantom ship!" Cecily said in a hushed voice.

The girls' hearts began to beat faster. Could they

believe their eyes? *Was* the story true? But where did the ghost ship come from?

Bess stuttered nervously, "I—I h-hope it doesn't come down here!"

Suddenly from the phantom craft came a scream of terror. The launch began to list. The next second all the lights went out and the boat vanished!

CHAPTER VII

The Bull's-Eye Window

BESS shrieked as the phantom launch disappeared underwater. "I've—I've never believed in ghosts," she said shakily, "but now I'm afraid I do!"

George looked at her scornfully. "Ghosts, nothing! There must be some logical explanation."

Cecily had little to say except that she was mighty glad the girls were with her. "I would have been terrified staying here alone!" she added. "I don't blame Henry Winch a bit for wanting to move."

Nancy suggested they go to bed early. "I don't believe the ghost ship will bother us," she said reassuringly.

The young sleuth did not say anything to the others but determined to get up early and investigate the far end of the lake to see if she could pick up any clues to the weird apparition. She awoke at daylight, dressed quickly, and slipped out of the cottage. Nancy followed the path along the water, and crossed the beach below the lodge. Then she set off through the woods. As she reached the area of fog, Nancy saw a swampy stretch before her.

"It won't hurt me to slosh through," she said to herself gamely. Holding her shoes, she waded in. "Why, the water's warm!" Her theory that there were probably hot springs in that section of the lake had proved to be correct.

The swamp was about three hundred feet long. It was more treacherous than Nancy had bargained for and she found herself floundering and slipping until she was soaking wet. The girl detective smiled.

"This is a crazy procedure," she told herself. "I haven't picked up one single clue, and what a mess I am!"

Nevertheless, Nancy pushed on and after a while reached dry land. The trees were thick here, but just beyond them was a large, relatively cleared area, with scrubby bushes and tall grass as well as a few saplings.

In the center of the clearing stood the tumbledown remains of an old-fashioned bandstand. Nancy examined the platform and the storage area underneath, but found nothing to suggest an answer to the phantom ship.

Disappointed, she turned back and reached the

cottage just as the other girls were getting up. They stared at her.

Nancy grinned. "Yes, I know I'm a sight. But it was all in the cause of trying to solve the mystery of that phantom ship. However, I learned absolutely nothing." She added laughingly, "It must rise out of the water, after all."

The others knew she was teasing and were sorry she had found no explanation. Cecily remarked, "I'll never feel completely safe here until that mystery is cleared up. Nancy, do you have some theory about it?"

The girl detective shrugged. "I've been wondering about those people at Pudding Stone Lodge. This ghost-ship business started after they moved there."

"You mean they could be connected in some way with the mirage or whatever it is?" asked George.

Nancy looked thoughtful. "It's a possibility. Anyhow, I'd like to do some investigating in the area of the lodge. Please don't mind if I skip helping with the dishes."

"Do you think you'll be safe alone?" Cecily asked fearfully.

Nancy assured her she would be and said she might be able to hide among the trees better if she were alone. She changed into dry clothes, and directly after eating, set off.

This time, Nancy chose a vantage point on the side of the house which faced the lake. Her attention was drawn to a third-floor window, called a bull's-eye window because of its roundness and small size.

Suddenly Nancy tensed. Sharp flashes of light were coming from the room where the bull's-eye window was. Apparently a mirror was being used to reflect sunlight.

Nancy watched intently to see if anyone would appear at the window, but no one did. "Maybe the pane is too high from the floor," she thought.

The young sleuth could well believe that something strange was going on inside the big stone house and even that someone was signaling for help. Her mind conjured up all sorts of possibilities about a prisoner who was bound and gagged in the room.

"I certainly can make a deep, dark mystery out of almost anything," she chided herself with a smile as she moved away. Nancy realized she had been gone from the cottage for some time and no doubt the other girls were eagerly awaiting her return so they might all go to town to start their investigating.

When Nancy arrived at the cottage, she heard Niko's hit record being played and realized Cecily must be using the cottage owner's phonograph.

"Sounds better than it did last night," Nancy

thought, walking in. She mentioned this to the others.

Cecily said it was her very own record which Niko had given her. Nancy, curious, went for her disc and put it on the player. It was good, but definitely not so clear-cut as the other.

"It does sound different," Cecily conceded. "Not so sharp. Sometimes it seems a bit fuzzy."

Nancy picked up the two records and compared them. Although at first glance they looked exactly the same, she noticed that the label on hers was paler than the other.

"These records have the same serial number," said Nancy, "but it's just possible the one I bought last night is a pirated recording."

"You mean," said Bess, her eyes opening wide in astonishment, "that someone is forging Niko's records and selling them?"

"It's possible," Nancy answered. "I think we should ask Eddie where he bought this supply of records. Also, I think you, Cecily, should telephone Niko's record company and tell them."

Nancy said she had still another suggestion. "Let's drive on to the county seat at Ridgeton. One of us can go to the courthouse and trace the ownership of Pudding Stone Lodge as far back as possible."

The other girls were ready, so as soon as Nancy showered and dressed for town, they set off. As they were driving past Henry Winch's dock, they saw the stocky man coming out of the rear of his store with a suitcase and an armful of clothes.

"He's leaving!" George exclaimed.

Nancy stopped and asked him if this were true and he said Yes, indeed—he was not going to stay in that haunted spot another night. She urged him not to be hasty, saying she was sure the girls would get to the bottom of the launch mystery soon.

"I sure wish you could," he answered. "I tell you it would save this lake as a summer resort."

Nancy smiled. "After all, Mr. Winch," she said, "no harm has come to you. Why not wait a few days? We're not far away if you need help."

"Well, I'll think about it," he said. "Maybe I won't go right now."

"I'd like to rent a canoe from you," Nancy went on. "I may want to inspect that phantom ship at close range."

A wild look came into Mr. Winch's eyes. "Don't, Miss Drew! It ain't safe! I'll leave a canoe at your cottage, but you'd better think twice, young lady, before you go up in that foggy area."

"All right, I will," Nancy promised.

When they reached the main road, Nancy stopped the car. "The county seat is to our left, and Misty Lake to our right. Why don't we go to Ridgeton first and see about an ironmonger, then stop at Eddie's on the way back?"

This was agreed upon and Nancy turned left. As they rode along, she told about the flashing light from the bull's-eye window of Pudding Stone Lodge. George said, "I believe it was just the sunlight glinting on the glass."

Cecily and Bess were inclined to think there was more to it, but could offer no explanation which Nancy had not already thought of.

When they reached the county courthouse, George offered to do the research work and try to find the identity of the original owner of Pudding Stone Lodge.

"Good," said Nancy. "Bess and I will inquire about an ironmonger while Cecily phones the record company."

The girls separated. Nancy made several inquiries and learned that a Mr. Finnerin was the present owner of an ironmongering establishment which had been in town for over a hundred years. The business was housed in a small building on a very narrow cobblestone street.

Mr. Finnerin said that unfortunately his old ledger had been destroyed by fire and he personally had no knowledge of the sale of any iron bird to Pudding Stone Lodge.

"But why don't you look around at some samples of our old-time work?" he suggested. "Maybe it will help you."

The company had set aside one room of old and

new products. The antique birds included cranes for the garden, and owls and eagles for roof cornices and door knockers.

"This is probably the type of thing we should look for," Bess whispered to Nancy, and her friend nodded.

The girls thanked Mr. Finnerin and walked back to a tearoom where the four girls had arranged to meet for luncheon. After they gave their orders, each told what she had found out. Cecily had still been unable to reach either Niko or the Waynes. She had had a talk with an official of the record company, however, and he had asked that someone bring the two records to their office in Baltimore.

"They're very much interested in your theory of piracy, Nancy," she said. "I think you should be the one to go."

"I'd be glad to. But let's decide tomorrow."

George said she had learned that the original owner of Pudding Stone Lodge was André Delaroy and it had been built in 1825. His two sons were Simon and William. She smiled at Cecily. "It sure looks as if Pudding Stone Lodge was really your ancestor's home."

Cecily was greatly excited, and listened intently as George went on, "The property was inherited by Simon Delaroy's only child, Ann. She married a Wayne."

"Oh, George, that's wonderful!" Cecily said, her eyes dancing. "We *are* looking in the right place for the iron bird! Just think! The old family treasure must be buried some place at the lodge. As soon as we finish eating, let's go back and make plans."

"But first we must stop at Eddie's Soda Shop," Nancy reminded her, "and find out the name of the jobber who supplied him with Niko's records."

When they reached the shop, Nancy suggested that they purchase some candy and nuts so that Eddie would not be suspicious. As he was filling the order, she asked casually, "By the way, Eddie, who supplies you with records?"

The soda-shop owner grinned. "I suppose you mean Niko's hit. I can get all you want. They come from a local jobber. His name is Neal Raskin."

"I don't need any more right now, but when I go home—" Nancy left the sentence unfinished. Quickly she consulted a telephone directory and found that Raskin's office was located near town, on the highway.

As the girls walked toward the car, Nancy said, "Cecily, why don't we drop you and George at Neal Raskin's office while Bess and I search again for the iron bird?"

"You'll come back to pick us up?"

"Yes."

Cecily said she was torn between two desires—to hunt for the bird and to help Niko. She finally agreed to go with George and find out more about the record.

Nancy and Bess drove off. "We'll leave the car at the cottage," said Nancy.

When they reached it, the girls were surprised to see a note tacked to the door. It said:

Come to lodge. Bird is found.
              K. Driscoll

CHAPTER VIII

Mean Relatives

"Our search is over!" said Bess. "Now we won't have to hunt for the iron bird after all."

Nancy frowned. "I don't trust Karl Driscoll. It would be dreadful if he has already opened the bird and found directions to the fortune! He may try to claim it."

"Cecily would be crushed," Bess commented.

The girls hurried outside. Nancy now noticed that the canoe had been delivered. Thinking she had better put the paddles in the cottage, she went down to the lake front. Tied to the paddles was a key and a note requesting that the canoe be returned to Winch's boathouse when the girls were finished with it. The key was to be left with Mrs. Hosking.

Nancy felt that the message also meant Henry Winch had decided to go away. "If I can only solve this mystery," she thought, "I'm sure he'll come back."

She put the paddles in the cottage and with Bess started off for Pudding Stone Lodge. They were met at the door by Karl Driscoll and his wife, who smiled upon being introduced to the girls. Both seemed very pleasant and told Nancy they had conducted a search and found an iron bird in a cellar storage room.

"This may be the one your friend is looking for," said Mr. Driscoll. "If so, you're welcome to take it. Follow me."

He led the way to the kitchen and opened a door to a darkened flight of steps leading below.

"There's no electricity down there, so take this flashlight with you. Walk straight ahead and you'll come to the storage room."

For an instant Nancy hesitated. Was this some kind of trick? She still did not like Karl Driscoll, despite his apparent friendliness. She wondered again about the strange humming noise which seemed to have come from the house. Then Nancy told herself, "Oh, I guess it will be all right." She took the light, and Bess followed her down the steep steps. A musty, moldering odor reached them.

"I wouldn't want to stay down here long," Bess remarked. "It's positively spooky."

They walked straight ahead and soon came to

a room with a sagging open door. One side was lined with shelves, the other full of hooks. On one of these hung a wall plaque of an iron bird. Nancy beamed the flashlight closely on it.

"Is this the one?" Bess asked.

"I doubt it—this doesn't strike me as very old," Nancy replied. "In fact, it looks like the one we saw last night in the window of the gift shop."

Nancy stood lost in thought. The suspicion crossed her mind that the Driscolls might have "planted" this bird, hoping to fool the girls so that they would take it away, and not come back to the lodge. Nancy played her light over the storage room. At the far end stood a large old-fashioned walnut chest of drawers. Above it she could just make out the outline of another door. Nancy wondered if this were a closed-off exit to the grounds.

"Let's go!" Bess urged. "This place gives me the creeps."

At the top of the cellar stairway, Mrs. Driscoll stood waiting for them. When Nancy said the iron bird was definitely not the right one, the woman looked disappointed.

"I'm so sorry. We hoped we had helped you in your search."

"Would you mind if we look other places in the house?" Nancy asked her.

"Why—uh—no," Mrs. Driscoll answered.

Nancy said she would like to go out on the roof.

"It is just possible I may find some evidence that an iron bird was once used as a cornice," she explained. Mrs. Driscoll agreed, though a bit reluctantly.

Bess spoke up. "How about my looking around the outside of the house at the door knockers and so forth? Then I'll walk back to the cottage and start supper."

"All right, but if I get too interested in my search, you'd better drive to town and pick up George and Cecily."

Bess nodded and went out the front door, as Mrs. Driscoll led Nancy up the stairs. They walked a short distance down a hallway past several rooms with closed doors until they reached one which the woman opened. It revealed the attic stairs.

At that moment Nancy heard children's voices. They were coming from one of the bedrooms.

"Your children?" she asked Mrs. Driscoll with a smile.

"Yes." An instant later the door burst open and identical twins—a boy and a girl about three years old—rushed out. Both were crying.

"Uncle Vince is mean!" the little girl sobbed.

"Yes, he is!" the little boy echoed. "We don't want to play with him!"

Mrs. Driscoll was annoyed. She grabbed the children and shoved them back into the room.

"Don't you dare leave here again!" she said angrily.

Taking the key from the inside of the door, she slammed it shut and locked it from the outside, pocketing the key. At once the children began to cry and scream loudly while kicking and banging on the door.

Nancy was appalled at such treatment and barely refrained from protesting. She wondered about the strange girl in the woods. Was she the Driscolls' nursemaid and where was she?

Mrs. Driscoll marched back along the hall to the attic stairway and told Nancy to go up. As she herself followed, Mrs. Driscoll explained that as a sideline the brothers had an acrobatic act. Vince was trying to teach the twins to perform and made them practice their stunts over and over again.

"You know how children are," Mrs. Driscoll said. "They'd rather just play."

Nancy made no comment. She felt that three years of age was pretty young for children to be handled in such a manner.

In the attic Nancy looked around for the bull's-eye window but did not see it. There were two regular-shaped windows, both of them too high up to reach. They cast a dim light around the place, which was filled with an assortment of old trunks and boxes.

Turning, Nancy noticed a closed door, which

evidently opened into a third-floor bedroom. That must be where the bull's-eye window was! She asked Mrs. Driscoll about this.

"Oh, you noticed that from the outside?" the woman queried. "Yes, that's where the circular window is. The room is locked. The owner keeps some things stored in there, I guess."

She showed Nancy a small door which opened onto a flat section of the roof with a low railing.

"I think what you have in mind, Miss Drew, is dangerous. But if you insist upon looking around, you can do so from here. As you can see, part of the roof is flat, but part is pretty steep. I warn you to watch your footing!"

Nancy promised she would do so and stepped outside. Mrs. Driscoll said she would go downstairs now and attend to the children.

From where she stood Nancy could see the entire lake and all the cottages which faced it. She saw Bess just entering the front door of the cottage.

"I guess she didn't find anything," thought Nancy.

She looked over as much of the roof as she could see, but there was nothing resembling an iron bird. Spotting a ladder against the chimney, toward the front of the house, Nancy climbed over the railing and carefully made her way down the sloping roof to the ladder. Quickly she climbed it, and holding onto the chimney for support, was able to view the entire layout of the roof. There was not a sign of a decorative bird in any section.

Nancy thought, "Maybe the bird isn't a fixed ornament, and Simon Delaroy hid it on the property." A worrisome thought struck her. What if someone had already located it?

Nancy climbed down the ladder, and made her way back to the attic door. To her amazement, it would not open.

"Oh, dear!" Nancy murmured. "I hope it's not one of those self-locking doors!"

She tugged and pushed, but the door would not budge. Had it locked automatically—or had the door been bolted from the inside by one of the Driscolls? And if so, what was the reason? The only explanation she could think of was that these mysterious people wanted to keep her out of the house until they had accomplished something about which they did not want her to know.

Nancy looked off into the distance, wondering if she could possibly signal Bess. But at that same moment she saw her friend come from the cottage, lock it, and then hurry up the path to where the car was parked. The faint sound of a motor came to Nancy's ears and she knew Bess had set off for the village.

Nancy tried the door once more with no luck. She began to pound on it loudly. She rapped until her knuckles were sore, but no one came to let her in. Maybe everybody had left the house, she thought.

Exasperated, Nancy began to cry out, "Help! Help! I'm locked out on the roof!"

She kept repeating her plea, but if anyone heard it, he had no intention of coming to her aid.

"I wonder if there's any way to get to the ground from here except through that door." Nancy walked toward the lake side of the house. She leaned over the railing and thought she saw what might be a fire escape. Here the roof sloped sharply. A drainpipe led down it to the gutter.

Nancy decided to lie flat on the roof and edge herself along, holding onto the pipe. If she were right about the fire escape, she could reach it from this angle. Her heart thumping, the young sleuth climbed over the railing and tested the drainpipe. It seemed to be firm.

Nancy let herself down the roof gingerly, and indeed found what was once a fire escape. But time and weather had loosened it from the wall. She knew it would be too hazardous to try climbing down. Besides, there was a ten-foot drop from the end of it to the ground. There was nothing to do but go back to the attic door. "I guess I'll have to break it down!" Nancy thought wryly.

When she reached the door, she blinked unbelievingly. It was open a crack!

"I didn't just dream it was locked," Nancy told herself. "Someone was playing a grim joke on me!"

She hurried down the attic stairs. As she started along the hall Nancy heard quarreling adult voices coming from one of the rooms near that of the twins'.

The next instant the door opened with a bang and Vince Driscoll stepped out. Seeing Nancy, the burly man seized the girl's arm roughly. His face was red with rage and fire seemed to leap from his eyes.

"What are you doing here?" he demanded.

CHAPTER IX

The Vandal

INDIGNANT, Nancy shook herself loose from Vince Driscoll's grasp. At that moment his sister-in-law came from the same room and glared at him. "Karl and I gave Miss Drew and her friends permission to come here and hunt for an iron bird," she said coldly.

"Why didn't you tell me?" Vince asked sullenly. "I'd have warned you not to. She's snoopy and a troublemaker." He turned to Nancy. "Don't show up here again!"

Mrs. Driscoll set her jaw firmly. "That's for Karl to decide, not you."

Vince seemed about to retort, but instead kept still and stalked on down the hall. Nancy then told Mrs. Driscoll about having been locked out. The woman said, "Vince didn't know you were here and went up to the attic. That door to the roof is not supposed to be open so he locked it. After a while I went up to see why you'd been there so long and found out what had happened. Since you weren't on the balcony I assumed you were somewhere on the roof, and unlocked the door."

"I appreciate that," said Nancy. "I could just picture myself staying out there all night!" She decided to make light of the matter and pretend that she accepted the explanation without question. But she was very suspicious.

Suddenly she thought of the closed-up room with the bull's-eye window. Had the Driscolls locked her out deliberately because they themselves had been keeping something—or someone—hidden in it? "And maybe moved out the person or object while I was outside," Nancy concluded. "It could even have been the red-haired girl. But what's the reason?"

Mrs. Driscoll escorted Nancy to the front door and said good-by pleasantly. "It's too bad the bird in the storage room isn't the one you're looking for," she said. "If we happen to come across another, we'll let you know."

"Thank you," Nancy said, and started down the road. The Driscoll family puzzled her. She wondered about the brothers' maintenance business. "They seem to be home a lot," Nancy thought. "Well, maybe they don't get many calls."

In any case, they certainly did not seem to get along well together!

"Could it be because of the twins?" Nancy reflected. "But why?"

She vividly recalled the hard look Karl Driscoll had given her in the general store. She was sure he was not pleased that the girls were living at the lake. "Though why did he go out of his way to be helpful?"

When Nancy reached the cottage the three girls came out to meet her and she reported her adventure.

Bess was concerned. "Why, Nancy, you might have slipped off that roof and been killed!"

Nancy grinned. "I guess I'm just a tough old sleuth," she answered.

"It's a good thing, because you're in for a surprise," George stated. "Wait until you see this cottage!"

As Nancy walked inside, she stared aghast at the scene before her. Tables and chairs had been broken. Every drawer in the place had been emptied of its contents, which were scattered around the floor. Bess had endeavored to put some of the things away before picking up the other two girls. The three had just started working again when Nancy arrived.

"It's vandalism!" Cecily said to Nancy. "Oh, who would want to do such a thing?"

"So far," said Bess, "we haven't found anything missing."

George nodded. "Some intruders are like that. They get so angry if they can't find what they're looking for, they'll tear a place to pieces."

The girls went on straightening up and repairing the furniture as best they could. As they worked, George and Cecily reported that they had gone to Neal Raskin's office, but he was not there. No one seemed to know where he had gone or when he would return.

Suddenly Bess said, "I'm starved! Do you realize it's seven o'clock? I never did start supper, what with this mess!"

The girls stopped working and by seven-thirty were seated around the little table, eating hungrily and chatting over the day's adventures.

"They all seem to add up to nothing," said Cecily, a sad expression in her eyes.

To cheer her, Nancy suggested taking a ride in the canoe. Cecily eagerly accepted.

"You two go," said George. "Bess and I will do the dishes."

Nancy and Cecily each took a paddle, and without even consulting each other, they found themselves heading for Pudding Stone Lodge.

By this time it was late dusk and a mist had begun to rise up from the water. In the foggy area it was thicker than ever.

"We'd better stay away from there," said Cecily. "We might get lost."

Pudding Stone Lodge was well lighted, and Nancy wondered what was going on inside the house.

Suddenly the strange humming noise came to the girls' ears. As before, its source was elusive, seeming to be outdoors, and yet muffled enough to be inside. "It might be some sort of generator in the house," said Nancy. "But I shouldn't think we'd notice it from here." The two girls listened intently but still could not figure out the exact location of the sound.

Cecily showed signs of apprehension. "We're pretty close to the place where that phantom boat appeared," she told Nancy. "Just in case there's something dangerous about it, don't you think we should leave?"

Personally Nancy would have liked to stay, but out of consideration for Cecily, she agreed. They turned the canoe around and began to paddle back toward the cottage. Nancy kept looking over her shoulder, hoping the apparition would appear. Cecily, on the other hand, was wishing just as hard that it would not. The lake remained dark.

When they reached the cottage dock, Nancy glanced up. She glimpsed a man's shadowy figure moving off among the trees around the cabin.

"The prowler!" Nancy thought.

She leaped from the canoe and made a wild dash after the man. But he began running too. There

Nancy dashed after the prowler

was enough light from the cottage and the rising moon to help Nancy keep track of the fleeing man. But he had too much of a head start and soon she lost sight of him completely.

"He certainly acted guilty," Nancy told herself.

Cecily had beached the canoe and was carrying the paddles to the cottage. Nancy met her. "What in the world made you dash off?" Cecily asked.

When Nancy explained, Cecily's eyelids flickered worriedly. She was silent as the two girls went inside. Nancy told Bess and George of her fruitless chase. Cecily kept clasping and unclasping her hands nervously. Nancy was about to try reassuring her when suddenly Satin aroused from a half-sleeping posture, arched his back, and stared into the next room, which was dark.

"What does he see?" Bess whispered.

Without warning, the cat shot into the room. There was a slight squeak and in a few seconds Satin emerged triumphantly, a mouse in his mouth! He placed it at Bess's feet.

"Oh, how horrible!" Bess cried out. "Take that thing away!"

Satin, as if he understood, carried the mouse back into the dark room. Unexpectedly Cecily smiled. "He's having himself a feast, I suppose."

George said, "I wish Satin had pounced on that vandal and sunk his teeth into the fellow!"

The girls laughed, then Cecily lapsed into her

unhappy mood. A few minutes later she arose. "I just can't stand not seeing or talking to Niko any longer! If you'll drive me to town, I'll catch the late bus for Baltimore, and maybe see the last part of his performance."

She consulted her watch and discovered that it would be nip and tuck as to whether she could make the bus in time. Nancy agreed to try. As Cecily tossed a few things into her suitcase, Bess and George declared that Nancy should not go alone.

"Your father wouldn't like it one bit," said George.

"We're going with you," Bess insisted, "vandal or no vandal."

Nancy hugged the cousins. "I'm sure it isn't necessary, but I love you both for it."

Cecily just managed to make the bus and everyone heaved a sigh of relief. Next, Nancy drove to the local police headquarters and went inside. Chief Stovall, a friendly, husky man, was on duty. She introduced herself and gave a quick report on the cottage entry. The chief listened attentively.

"We have a very limited force here, Miss Drew," he said. "But we'll do our best to nab the prowler. Offhand, I can't think of anyone I'd suspect among our villagers."

Nancy's thoughts flashed to the Driscolls—but she had no proof of her suspicions about them, and said nothing. She mentioned having seen the phantom launch.

Chief Stovall grinned. "I've heard those reports, and I certainly don't disbelieve you, Miss Drew. I've been out to the lake several evenings, for that purpose. But until I see it for myself, there is nothing I can do."

"I understand." Nancy smiled, and said good night. She, Bess, and George returned to the cottage, wondering in what kind of condition they would find it. Fortunately, no one had broken in, and the three friends settled down to read and write letters.

Satin, too, had curled up by the fire, which was now burning brightly. But suddenly he stood up and stared at the outside door.

George grinned. "Bess, maybe he's going to get you another mouse."

But her grin faded as the silence outside was broken. The girls heard the porch step creak.

CHAPTER X

An Exciting Find

LIKE a flash Nancy was at the front door of the cottage. She flung it open. A handsome, blond young man stood there, his hand lifted as if to knock.

"Niko Van Dyke!" she cried out involuntarily.

He smiled broadly. "You recognize me?"

Nancy, smiling, said, "I not only recognize you, but I'm terribly relieved to see you. Please come in."

"You mean you thought I was a burglar?" Niko asked as they all took seats.

"Well, we had a prowler here today who did a lot of damage and I was afraid he might be returning."

To Nancy's surprise, the young musician said, "I saw him, but I didn't know that he had already broken into the cottage. He was carrying an ax.

When he spotted me, he ran off toward the misty end of the lake."

"You saw him!" Bess exclaimed, coming forward. "What did he look like?"

When Niko described the man, Nancy looked at the other two girls significantly. He must be Vince Driscoll!

"What time did you see him?" Nancy asked.

When Niko told her, Nancy realized that Vince had rushed over to the cottage while she was locked on the roof—and before Bess's return—and damaged its contents. This must mean that the Driscolls were trying to frighten the girls away from the area.

Suddenly Nancy realized that Niko no doubt was looking for Cecily. Quickly she introduced herself and the others, then explained how they happened to be staying there.

"Cecily isn't here now?" Niko asked, a look of disappointment on his face.

"She's on her way to Baltimore," Nancy replied.

"Baltimore! But why?"

"To see you," Nancy replied. "It's a shame—you just missed her. We put her on the bus not long ago."

"Is she coming back here?" Niko asked.

Nancy nodded. "She has been trying day and night to get you on the phone."

"I've been pretty much tied up," Niko explained. "I wanted to come here as soon as I got Cecily's message, but this is the first chance I've had. The Flying Dutchmen are taking a night off. I've been very upset. Cecily may have told you that we had a disagreement and I felt pretty bad about it."

Somewhat embarrassed, Niko admitted that upon arriving at the village that afternoon he had walked for hours along the lake trying to think of a way to persuade Cecily to marry him right away. It was during that time he had seen the suspected vandal.

"If only I'd come directly here! But I hesitated, not knowing just how Cecily felt," Niko added dejectedly.

Nancy smiled sympathetically. "Cecily is very eager to get things straightened out too. That's one reason why I'm relieved to see you. Now I have a chance to tell you this."

Niko's sad expression vanished. Suddenly he looked happy and boyish. "I'm crazy about Cecily and want to marry her soon."

"She told us that too," said Bess. "We three hope she'll change her mind and not put off the wedding too long. Of course you know about the iron bird. We've all been helping her look for it, but haven't had any luck so far. There seems to be a mystery connected with the house and grounds where we think the bird is."

George spoke up. "But Nancy will solve it. She's a detective and a very good one."

Niko looked surprised. "I've never met a girl detective before, I sure wish you luck on this case. Cecily wants to find the fortune for us, but I keep telling her I can earn enough, and we don't have to live in grand style."

Nancy and her friends were impressed by the young man's sincerity. George spoke up. "Are you staying in town tonight or going back to Baltimore?"

"I'm staying at Mrs. Hosking's guest house," he replied. "But I must leave tomorrow morning."

A mischievous look suddenly came into Niko's eyes. "I tell you what. I'll come back here tomorrow night after our performance. But don't tell Cecily when she returns. I'd rather surprise her."

The girls promised, then Niko went on, "How would you three like to bring your dates and be my guests at our performance day after tomorrow?"

"Oh, we'd love it!" Bess burst out. "I'm dying to hear you and your band."

George added, "Your new record is neat!"

"It certainly is," Nancy agreed. "That's one reason Cecily was trying so hard to talk with you. We've found out your new record has been pirated!"

"What!" the musician cried out.

Nancy told the story and Niko frowned. He said, "I'm glad to learn that my record company is honest. I'm sure they'll sue this pirate immediately. Who is he?"

"We're not sure," Nancy replied. "We have one lead. We're going to follow it up in the morning and hope we'll have news for you tomorrow night. We've notified your record company and are going to take the two records to them."

Niko said he was very grateful for the girls' help. Bess insisted he stay and have some refreshment, and quickly served cookies and bottles of soda.

The foursome continued to discuss the mysteries as they ate, then Niko Van Dyke said good night.

As the girls were getting ready for bed, Bess said, "I almost wish I hadn't promised not to tell Cecily that Niko was here. I just know I'll have to bite my tongue half a dozen times before he gets back."

The others smiled, saying it was going to be difficult for them also.

In the morning the girls were up early, and drove to the village. The first thing they did was telephone their friends Ned, Burt, and Dave and invite them to Baltimore for Niko's performance. The three boys eagerly accepted, since their college term had not yet started. They would drive and plans were made for meeting in Baltimore.

Ned Nickerson had been a friend of Nancy's for some time. Burt Eddleton dated George, and Dave Evans was Bess's favorite escort.

Nancy and the cousins now headed for the highway, and Neal Raskin's office. This was in the warehouse of an electrical appliance factory, one of several manufacturing plants in the area. Nancy parked in the appliance factory's lot and went in to the warehouse office alone. Upon inquiring, she found that Raskin was still away.

"I understand he sells records,' Nancy said to the office clerk. "Would it be possible to look at a catalogue or list of what he has in stock?"

The young woman shook her head. "Mr. Raskin keeps his affairs to himself. When he leaves he locks up his office and nobody around here has the key to it."

Nancy thanked her and went outside to the car. As she got behind the wheel, the young sleuth reported what she had learned.

"Sounds suspicious to me," George remarked. "He's probably out delivering more of those phony records."

"Of course we have no proof of this," Nancy reminded her. She turned the car and started back for Misty Lake village. Just then a slow-moving oil truck came toward her. Behind this, and honking impatiently, was another truck. As Nancy pulled opposite it and glanced at the driver, she recognized him as Vince Driscoll. He looked over at her, scowled, and drove on.

"I wonder where he is going," Nancy said.

"Probably to service one of these factories around here," Bess remarked.

George said, "I think we ought to report him to the police. They could hold him until Niko gets back and can identify him as the man who broke into our cottage."

Nancy disagreed. "We'd feel pretty foolish if Vince was not the vandal," she said. "Then the Driscolls would make our sleuthing harder than ever for us."

"I guess you're right," George conceded. "But don't forget, Niko said that when the man ran away from the cottage, he went toward the lodge."

Nancy said she thought as soon as they got back they should make another visit to the foggy area to look for clues to the phantom launch, but this time they would do it secretly. They would hike along the path through the woods near the lake front.

"Let's have lunch in the village," Nancy proposed. "I want to stop in that gift shop where they had the iron bird."

"To find out if Karl Driscoll bought it?" Bess guessed.

"Yes."

As soon as the girls finished eating, they went to

ask the gift-shop owner about the iron bird they had seen in the window.

"A man bought it," was his reply.

On a hunch Nancy described Karl Driscoll.

"That's the one," the man said.

The trio drove home. Nancy, although excited about this clue, kept wondering what Karl's motive was. Did he hope to find the real iron bird? Or did he wish to keep the girls away from the lodge for some other reason? There were so many angles to the mystery—if she could only solve one!

When the girls reached the cottage, they found Cecily there. She was depressed, reporting that she had missed Niko in Baltimore. "No one knew where he was." The red-haired girl's voice trembled. "At first I thought of staying longer, but then I began to think probably he didn't want to see me again, so I came back."

Bess put her arms around the girl. "Now listen, Cecily," she said, "Niko is—" Bess caught herself just in time. "You mustn't lose heart. Niko loves you, I know."

"Oh, I want to believe that!" Cecily said.

She turned down the girls' invitation to go with them on the hike up the lake. Nancy, Bess, and George changed into blue jeans, shirts, and hiking shoes. They started out at a brisk pace. When they reached the swampy area, the afternoon sun was already waning.

"We can't go much farther and get back before dark," Bess reminded the others.

Nancy was hardly listening. She had noticed a shabby rowboat half hidden in the mud among the reeds. It had not been there on her former visit! All three girls took off their shoes, and carrying them, waded in to look at the boat. This might be a clue to one of the mysteries!

"I see something!" Nancy exclaimed.

She reached inside the boat and picked up a small shiny object. Dangling from a bracelet was half of a heart-shaped gold locket!

CHAPTER XI

The Treacherous Slope

THE gold half-locket looked like Cecily's. "And this one is in perfect condition!" Nancy exclaimed. "So it hasn't lain in the boat very long."

"Do you think it belongs to that girl who looks like Cecily?" Bess asked.

"Yes, I do," Nancy answered. "Especially since I believe the two are related."

George was impatient for action. "I'll bet that girl could clear up a lot of mysteries if we could only find her again."

Nancy's thoughts were in a whirl. Why had the red-haired young woman seemed so frightened and run from the girls the first night at the cabin? "And why did she think we wanted to take the babies?" Nancy mused.

If the girl was related to Cecily, and she too had been searching around Pudding Stone Lodge for the family fortune, why had not Nancy and her friends seen her on the grounds?

Finally Nancy said, "The girl may come back here for the locket. Let's wait."

"But she may run away again if she sees us here," George argued.

"We'll hide," said Bess. "I don't like this soggy old place. Let's go up in the woods where it's dry."

Nancy decided to take the locket with her. If its owner did not appear, at least the young sleuth would have a valuable bit of evidence to show Cecily. The three girls sloshed out of the swamp, dried their feet, and put on their shoes. They climbed a steep slope and found a grassy spot among the trees from where they had a view of the rowboat. After fifteen minutes had gone by, George became restless.

"We might have to wait for ages," she said. "The girl may not have been wearing the bracelet. Perhaps it dropped out of her pocket or purse and she won't miss it for some time."

"That's possible," Nancy agreed. "Well, let's wait for half an hour more. If nothing happens, we'll leave." The girl detective's mind continued to dwell on all the possible clues they had uncovered so far. She had not forgotten the flashing light from the bull's-eye window at the lodge which she still believed was a signal.

Nancy sat up straight. Certain pieces of the mystery puzzle were beginning to fit into place. "Maybe it's too fantastic, but it *is* a pattern."

"Detective Drew," George said, "don't keep your deductions a secret."

Nancy smiled, then said somberly, "There might be something more sinister to this whole thing than we imagined."

"Like what?" Bess asked, wide-eyed.

"Well, that red-haired girl may not show up because she might have been kidnapped."

"Kidnapped! By whom?"

"The Driscolls."

Bess gasped. "What makes you think that?"

Quickly Nancy revealed her recent speculations. "And," she went on, "I'm sure the Driscolls are involved in something underhanded, and that their service business is a front."

George caught the drift of Nancy's thoughts. "You mean that this girl may have been searching around Pudding Stone Lodge and have discovered something crooked about the Driscolls? They caught her and are holding her prisoner to keep her from revealing it?"

"Exactly."

George whistled. "This mystery sure is getting complicated. Now Nancy has put kidnappers into the picture."

Nancy laughed. "I didn't say I know this is

true," she defended herself. "I was just thinking out loud."

"I like it," said Bess. "Tell us some more of your thoughts."

Nancy went on, "You remember that machine noise—well, it could be from a printing press—the Driscoll brothers may even be counterfeiters."

"You mean you and I were in the house of people who are trying to cheat Uncle Sam?" Bess inquired.

Again Nancy chuckled. "You asked me to think out loud, Bess. Have you had enough of the awful possibilities?"

Bess looked hurt. "I can take it, but I really think that if any of these ideas you mentioned have any truth in them, the police should be notified."

"Without one shred of evidence?" Nancy asked. "No, I won't make any accusations at this point. But I'm going to prove or disprove my theories."

George stood up. She glanced at her watch and said, "The half hour is up, and if that red-haired gal *is* a prisoner, she's not going to come around here. Let's go!"

In her haste George stepped backward down the slope and lost her balance. She teetered for several seconds as both Nancy and Bess made a dive for her. But they could not reach the swaying girl in time. She fell on her back, hitting her head hard. The blow stunned her, and George began to roll down the hill.

Nancy and Bess gasped. Their friend was heading straight for a group of thorny bushes at the bottom!

The two girls leaped forward but were too late. Bess screamed as her dazed cousin hurtled into the bushes. Fortunately, her body had swerved and landed feet first. This saved her face and hands from being scratched.

By the time Nancy and Bess reached her, George was coming out of her daze.

"Thank goodness!" Bess heaved a sigh of relief, and pulled George from the bushes. Her legs were badly scratched and her clothes dirty and torn.

Bess rushed over to the water and soaked a handkerchief, which she brought back and laid across George's eyes and forehead. The dark-haired girl sat up. "What a ninny I am!" she exclaimed. "Well, at least I can wash my face and hands."

Bess insisted upon getting fresh water and doing the washing. George smiled. "I have to admit sometimes you treat me pretty well, cousin," she teased.

Bess made a face, then went again to the lake, and after the third cleanup George began to look more like herself. There was a slight lump on the back of her head, but she said it was not really bothering her.

"But I would appreciate going back to the cottage," she said.

George objected to being helped, but Nancy and Bess paid no attention to her protests. "We don't want any more spills," Bess told her.

When they reached the cottage, George refused to lie down, saying what she needed was a good, juicy steak.

Cecily, after expressing her sympathy over George's accident, offered to get supper. "We do have steak and it won't take long to broil it."

Nancy offered to help, saying she had a surprise for Cecily and would tell her about it while they were working in the kitchen. She pulled the half-locket from her pocket.

"This matches yours, doesn't it?" she asked.

Cecily stared unbelievingly. "I'm sure it does, but I'll get mine and we'll compare."

There was excitement all over again when Cecily put the two halves together. A perfect fit! "Where in the world did you get this?" she asked.

Nancy told the whole story, adding that during her previous visit to the area the old battered boat had not been there. "Either someone just tried to hide it, or it drifted there. I'm sure the locket wasn't in it very long. I do have an idea as to the person who lost the locket."

"Who?" Cecily asked eagerly.

Nancy reminded her of the hunch that the red-haired girl who resembled Cecily was a relative. "And if this part of your great-grandmother's locket does belong to her, I'm convinced."

"Oh, I must meet my double!" Cecily cried excitedly. "It's exasperating that we can't find her or the iron bird. What do you think we should do next?" she asked Nancy.

The young sleuth said she had no solution except hard work, meaning that they would have to keep on searching around Pudding Stone Lodge.

Cecily was silent for a full minute before she remarked, "That other red-haired girl's actions have been so strange I'm sure she's very worried about something. I wish I could help her!"

Nancy confided the theory that she had expressed to Bess and George.

"Oh, dear!" Cecily exclaimed. "If that girl is a prisoner, and you didn't hear or see anything of her when you were in the lodge, she must be well hidden."

"I agree," Nancy replied. "Of course she might have been taken out of the house and been kept somewhere else until after I'd gone."

During the delicious steak supper, which Cecily and Nancy served, the girls continued to talk about the locket, the missing red-haired girl, and Pudding Stone Lodge.

When they finished eating, George declared she felt fine and again longed for action. Bess looked at her cousin sternly. "No physical exercise tonight. But I'll make a bargain with you. I'll drive you to the movies over at Ridgeton."

"Neat idea," said George. "I accept."

Bess turned to Nancy meaningfully. "I hope you girls don't mind not being invited. Somebody probably should be here to guard this cottage."

The significance of Bess's remark was not lost on Nancy. They must keep Cecily at the cottage so that she would surely be there when Niko came!

"How about a little walk?" Nancy asked Cecily.

"Oh, I don't believe so," the other girl answered. "I'd like to write some letters. My friends will wonder what has happened to me."

Nancy asked if Cecily minded if she went out by herself for a short time.

Cecily said, "Oh, go right ahead. I think I'll lock myself in, though, in case there are any prowlers around. When you return, knock three times."

Bess and George went off in the car, while Nancy strode along the lake front. Before she knew it, she had reached the path leading to Pudding Stone Lodge. On a sudden hunch Nancy decided to climb quietly up along the slope and pick up any clues she could. As she walked toward the house and looked upward, the young sleuth stopped short.

There was a steady glow of light from the bull's-eye window!

CHAPTER XII

Precarious Hiding Place

THE light from the bull's-eye window began to flash on and off. Surely this must be a signal, Nancy thought.

She ducked behind a large bush and looked around uneasily. It occurred to her that a sudden light beamed on the grounds could reveal her hiding place. Nancy began to count the flashes to see if they spelled an SOS message. But they did not.

"I may be letting my imagination run away with me," she told herself. "It could be that the owner himself came back to find something in that room, and is poking a flashlight into various places. That would make it seem as if a light were going on and off."

Nancy's keen instinct told her, however, that

this was not the right explanation. There were too many other suspicious and mysterious goings-on in connection with the Driscoll property! As she stood gazing, suddenly a light went on in the kitchen. Was someone getting a snack? Nancy decided to take a chance and move closer. She was too far below the kitchen windows to see anyone inside. But she did hear a door slam. Had someone gone to the cellar? Nancy listened for the person's return. After a time, when she heard nothing, she began to wonder if the Driscolls carried on some kind of work down there.

It occurred to Nancy that the signaling from the window might have been for someone waiting on the lake or in the woods—or, as she had guessed earlier, from a prisoner in the room. At that moment she heard a muffled humming sound.

"It's the same machine noise that I heard before!" Nancy thought.

She decided to try tracing it. Straining her ears, the young sleuth followed the sound down through the woods of the embankment. It was now bright moonlight and she had no trouble descending. As Nancy neared the beach, she was startled by a rustle of the brush behind her. She darted in back of a large tree, hoping no one was following. The rustling had stopped. There was complete silence now, except for the humming sound. Nancy took a chance and moved toward the beach.

Suddenly she stopped, her heart beating faster. She noticed the silhouettes of two men standing not far from the water. Where had they come from?

Now the humming noise was louder. The girl detective was sure she was near its source. Nancy was greatly puzzled. What *was* the source of the sound?

Suddenly the men turned and walked directly toward Nancy. One of them was Vince Driscoll, the other a stranger, short, wiry, and partially bald.

Hastily Nancy retreated along the woods path. She looked back. The men had begun to climb the bluff. With a sigh of relief, Nancy paused. But the next moment the men stopped too. "She's here somewhere," said the stranger. "Karl saw her!"

Nancy tried to figure out who "she" might be. "Do they mean me, or the mysterious red-haired girl?"

Then she heard Vince say, "Come on. Let's look over here." Again they started in Nancy's direction.

Sure she was in danger, the young sleuth tiptoed away. But she stepped squarely on a dead branch, snapping it with a loud *crack*.

"What was that?" she heard Vince growl. "Somebody's ahead of us."

The men broke into a run, and Nancy had no

choice but to run herself. Could she make her way to the cottage safely? A chilling thought struck her. The men might have a confederate searching the woods! She could be trapped!

Wondering what her best means of escape might be, Nancy decided on Henry Winch's dock. This was now not far away.

"I can lower myself under it and hang on," thought Nancy. "If necessary, I can even drop into the water."

As quietly as she could, Nancy continued running. But Vince and his companion evidently could hear her for they hurried in the same direction.

Nancy managed to reach Henry Winch's store. She dashed around the side which was in the shadow and let herself down underneath the dock. She clung to a supporting beam.

A minute later her pursuers stomped onto the dock. "I caught a glimpse of her," the stranger said. "She's got to be around here somewhere."

As Nancy's heart pounded, the two searchers circled the little building. She heard Vince say he would try the door and windows.

"They're locked!" he growled in disgust.

"Maybe she had a key. Why don't you bust in and find out?" the other man asked.

In a moment Nancy heard the tinkle of glass and the raising of a window sash. There was silence for several seconds, then Vince's voice. "She's not in here. You weren't seeing things, were you, Webby?"

"I sure wasn't," his companion answered angrily. "Hey! Maybe she's underneath this dock. Let's look."

Nancy had just decided that there was nothing left for her to do but drop underwater and hold her breath as long as she could, when a sharp whistle pierced the air from the direction of Pudding Stone Lodge.

"That's Karl!" Vince exclaimed. "Wonder what's up."

"We'd better go," Webby said.

To Nancy's intense relief, the two men rushed off. She lost no time in hoisting herself up from under the dock and watched the men run along the beach. To her astonishment, when they reached the bluff just below Pudding Stone Lodge, the two disappeared!

"Is there an exit to the beach from the cellar of the house?" Nancy thought excitedly. "Old houses often had secret passages to be used as hiding places in time of trouble."

Nancy also decided that it was possible the machine that made the humming noise was in this very same passageway! But what was the machine for? Her mind went back to the counterfeit idea.

"Oh, dear, if I could only find out!"

At that very moment she heard a ship's bell ring. The girl detective stood stock-still, listening. The ringing continued for about a minute. Then suddenly in the fog at the end of the lake, the phantom launch appeared!

"This time I'm going to find out what's going on!" Nancy determined.

Leaving the dock, she sped to the Baker cottage. She pounded on the door, calling, "Quick, Cecily! Let me in!"

Cecily dashed to the door and opened it. "What's the matter?" she asked.

"The phantom launch! Look!"

Cecily stepped to the porch and stared at the weird sight. Nancy, meanwhile, grabbed a paddle. "I'm going to try and find out what it is!" she cried, and rushed down to the canoe.

Nancy turned it over, pushed the craft into the water, and jumped in. She began to stroke furiously toward the phantom boat.

The shortest route was by the center of the lake where the water was deepest. The canoe glided forward at racing speed. Nancy had been so intent upon the sight ahead that she failed to notice the craft was leaking. Now she felt her ankles getting wet and looked down in dismay. Water was pouring into the canoe.

"What horrible luck!" Nancy murmured in disgust. "Just when I had the mystery in my grasp."

All the young sleuth could do was gaze ahead and try to get as clear a picture of the phantom launch as she could.

Suddenly a black cloud blotted out the moon. When it reappeared, the launch had vanished, and within seconds, the canoe sank!

CHAPTER XIII

A Spy?

STILL clutching her paddle, Nancy started to swim for land.

"I'm sure I couldn't rescue the canoe. It will have to be fished out of the bottom of the lake."

As Nancy neared shore, she began to wonder whether someone was waiting in ambush. There was no doubt in her mind that the canoe had been sabotaged! It had been all right when Henry Winch left it.

"Could it be the work of the Driscoll brothers?" she asked herself, and clutched the paddle tighter. "If anybody tries to waylay me I'll use this as a weapon!"

Before leaving the water, Nancy looked up and down the narrow beach, at the foot of Pudding Stone Lodge. There was no one in sight and finally she stood up and waded ashore. A chill breeze struck her and she began to shiver.

"Great!" Nancy said to herself. "Whoever my enemies are they're tricky. It never occurred to me that anyone would tamper with the canoe."

Partly to keep from being seen and partly to keep out of the wind, Nancy went up to the path that led through the woods and headed for the cottage.

"If I weren't so uncomfortable and didn't have so much on my mind," Nancy thought, "I could really enjoy this gorgeous moonlight and scenery."

Suddenly, as she rounded a bend in the path, she saw a girl ahead.

"Cecily!" she cried out.

Instead of answering, the young woman fled up the hill among the trees. Nancy knew now that she was not Cecily but the other red-haired girl.

"Please wait! I want to talk to you!" she called. "I'm not going to harm you."

The fleeing girl paid no attention. Soon not even her footsteps could be heard. Where had she gone? To Pudding Stone Lodge?

Nancy became lost in speculation as she went on toward the cottage. Maybe she was wrong about the strange girl. If the young woman was afraid to speak to Nancy, she might well be a spy for the Driscolls—not a prisoner! Possibly she had been posted near the girls' cottage that evening, to follow anyone who came out.

Nancy pursued her line of reasoning. "As soon

as I set off in the canoe she could have run along the path, to see what happened to me. When the canoe filled with water and I began swimming, she knew I wasn't going to drown. She waited to see what I'd do when I got to shore. The instant I called out Cecily's name, that girl rushed back and reported everything to the Driscolls."

Another idea occurred to Nancy—that someone wanted to keep people from getting too close to the phantom ship, so he had sabotaged her canoe.

By the time Nancy reached the cottage, she was cold and exhausted. She saw smoke coming from the fireplace chimney and took heart at the thought of its cheering warmth.

As Nancy opened the door and walked in, she saw Bess, George, Cecily, and Niko grouped around a roaring fire.

"Nancy! Whatever happened to you?" Bess cried out, upon seeing the bedraggled, shivering girl.

Her friend normally would have given a humorous answer, but instead she said seriously, "Hello, Niko! I'm glad to see you again. As for me, somebody put a hole in the canoe and I took an unexpected bath."

"Who would have done that?" George asked. "Oh, don't tell us now, Nancy. You get yourself into a hot bath pronto!"

Nancy was glad to obey. Later, while she was dressing, Bess and George came into her room. They had decided to retire, and leave Cecily and Niko alone to talk over their problems.

"Nancy," said George, "we were just about to send a search party out for you. Now, give us the details."

When Nancy finished her story, the cousins shook their heads ruefully. Bess said, "This mystery gets more dangerous all the time for you, Nancy. And here you are worrying about losing the canoe! It's just lucky you weren't drowned! I honestly don't think your father or Mrs. Gruen would want you to take such chances."

The young sleuth smiled. "But I never know when I'm going to have to take chances!" she countered. "I just know that any time I undertake a case, I'm apt to run into some kind of a trap."

"I suppose you're right," Bess conceded. "But I'm going to do my best to keep you out of any traps from here in!"

"Thanks, Bess," Nancy said with an affectionate look at her friend. "And now, about that other red-haired girl. I have two completely opposite ideas about her. One is that she is in cahoots with the Driscolls in some underhanded scheme; the other is that she's their prisoner or is somehow in their power. For example, it might be she managed to escape tonight. But she thinks that *I* am working with the Driscolls and only wanted to delay her so she could be recaptured."

Bess sighed. "You're going too fast for me, Miss Detective."

George spoke up. "For that matter, I wonder how other facets of the mysteries may involve this strange girl—such as the phantom launch, the peculiar humming noise, and even the treatment those poor twins are apparently getting!"

Bess shook her head. "I can't tax my brain any more tonight. Say, I'm starved! How about the three of us transferring to the kitchen for a midnight snack?"

Nancy chuckled. "To tell the truth, I think a little food would completely revive me. I've worked up an appetite by my long swim and hike."

Bess, the culinary expert, was out of the door by this time and heading for the little kitchen. The others followed.

"Well, what shall it be?" Bess held up a spoon and struck a chef-like pose.

"Hot tomato soup," said Nancy, "with cream in it."

"Sounds good," said George. "I'll make some toast to go with it."

"Anybody want a hamburger?" Bess giggled. "I'm going to make one for myself."

Suddenly Nancy felt ravenous and said she would have one too. "Make it three." George grinned. In a few moments Bess had the burgers sizzling in a pan.

Bess had just flipped them over when there came a tremendous *crash* from the living room!

CHAPTER XIV

The Cricket Clue

ALL three girls dashed into the living room. They looked horrified at the scene before them. The front door stood open, a huge rock lay on the floor and beside it both Cecily and Niko lay unconscious! Bess gave a little scream as she and George ran forward to kneel beside the striken couple.

Nancy was torn momentarily between helping them and trying to find the rock thrower. She rushed from the cottage and gazed around. Two men were racing along the lake front toward the lodge, and in a minute vanished from sight among the trees.

"I'll bet they're the Driscoll brothers!" Nancy murmured to herself. "I wish I'd had a better look. Well, I can't do anything about it now." She hurried back inside the cottage. For the first time she realized exactly what had happened. The two assailants had carried the heavy rock up to the porch, quietly opened the door, and thrown their weapon with full force at the couple. Cecily and Niko had been seated on the small couch before the fireplace, their backs to the door. Fortunately, the rock had struck the couch, but the force of the blow had pitched the pair forward, and they had struck their heads on the edge of the hearth.

"They might have fallen right into the fire!" Nancy thought, shuddering.

Bess and George were already giving Cecily and Niko first aid and in a little while they revived. Both had bruises on their heads, but otherwise were not injured. They were thunderstruck to learn what had happened.

"I think you need a police guard at this place," Niko said shakily.

Cecily looked wan and upset. Luckily there was a diversion at that moment. Bess cried out, "Oh, our hamburgers!" She dashed into the kitchen and presently announced that she had three very well-done, somewhat burned, hamburgers for sale.

Nancy, Bess, and George temporarily had lost their appetites. But there was enough of the hot soup for everyone and Bess served cups of it in the living room. As the group sat around sipping the soup, they discussed the mystery. None could think of any reason for the attack.

Presently Niko admitted to being very tired, and said he would drive back to Mrs. Hosking's for a good night's sleep.

"I'll see you all in the morning. How about Cecily driving to Baltimore with me tomorrow, and you other girls coming in Nancy's car? We can stop at my record company first."

The plan was agreed upon. As Niko was about to leave, Cecily said, "I'll have to do something with Satin while we're away. Will you ask Mrs. Hosking if she will keep him?"

Niko scooped up the beautiful black cat. "I'll take him right now. Good night, everybody."

Nancy was the first one awake the next morning. She hurried into the kitchen, and by the time the others opened their eyes, the delicious aroma of broiling bacon reached them. The girls took a quick dip in the lake, then ate before dressing. By nine o'clock they had locked the cottage and were on their way. While the others waited at Mrs. Hosking's, Nancy drove to police headquarters and talked with Chief Stovall. She told of the many happenings in or near the cottage since the prowler had broken in.

The chief frowned. "Last night's attack is certainly bad business. I'm sorry we've made no progress on catching the vandal. I take it you believe the same person—or persons—are responsible for both incidents. But this business about the phantom boat I still can't swallow. There must be some logical explanation for it."

Nancy smiled. "The apparition *is* pretty weird—but it is very lifelike."

"I just don't see any sense to it," the officer said. "Granted, this phantom ship is man-made, as you say. But who would want to do it and why?"

"To scare people away from the lake."

Chief Stovall shrugged. "Well, all right, I'll look into that, too," he promised, then the young sleuth left.

Nancy followed Niko's car all the way to Baltimore. When they reached the historic old city, she was glad the young musician was leading her through the tricky narrow one-way streets to the record company's office.

Niko introduced the girls to the president, Mr. Carpenter, and he in turn introduced another man as Police Detective Morton.

Nancy brought out the record she had purchased at the Misty Lake soda shop. She requested that before having it played, Mr. Carpenter bring in one of their own recordings of Niko's number. This was done and it was played from beginning to end as everyone listened carefully.

"It's a wonderful record!" Bess said dreamily.

"Thank you," Mr. Carpenter answered, smiling. "We think so too. And evidently the public does."

Nancy's record was now placed on the player. Again everyone listened intently. For the first time Nancy detected certain faint sounds on the disc which she had not noticed before. "It sounded just like crickets in the background," she exclaimed when the music came to an end.

Mr. Carpenter's jaw set grimly. "There's no question but that this was pirated from ours! Now we have something concrete. We'll go after these thieves!"

"How will you do it?" Niko asked.

Detective Morton spoke up. "I'll try tracing them through the jobber," he said.

Nancy gave Neal Raskin's name, explaining that the girls had tried unsuccessfully to see him. She suggested that the strange background noise on the record which sounded like crickets might be a clue, although a slight one, to the place in which the records were being cut.

"I realize," Nancy added, "that crickets are found throughout the country."

Detective Morton smiled at her. "Your suggestion may still be helpful, Miss Drew. At least it tells us the record was cut in a rural area where the sound of crickets could be plainly heard. And it must have been cut recently, since Niko's number came out last month. If you unearth any more good leads, please get in touch with me." Nancy promised to do so.

The callers arose and said good-by to Mr. Carpenter and the detective. The company president assured Niko everything would be worked out fairly, and he was glad to have proved to the young man that royalties were not being withheld from him.

"We'll start a suit against those pirates immediately!" Mr. Carpenter said.

"I sure hope you do." Niko replied. "Cecily and I need the money—to get married!"

Mr. Carpenter congratulated the engaged couple and wished them luck. "Maybe my engagement present to you will be a big fat royalty check!"

When he reached the street, Niko said he must go to the theater immediately for a rehearsal. He would see them after the show that evening.

When the singer had left, Bess asked Nancy, "What's next on our schedule?"

The girl detective said she thought they should locate the Kenneth Wayne home and see what they could find out. After getting directions from a policeman, Nancy drove there. The address they sought proved to be a modest apartment house. Nancy rang the bell marked *Wayne*, but there was no answer.

"How am I ever going to find out about these people?" Cecily asked.

"Somebody here must know them," said Nancy.

She rang the bell of a Mrs. Rumsey on the first floor.

The woman was very cooperative. She kept staring at Cecily as she replied to Nancy's question, "Mr. and Mrs. Wayne died about three years ago. Their two sons still rent the apartment, but both are in the Navy now and rarely come home."

The woman went on, "Also, there's a daughter named Susan. She was married in the old Wayne homestead up at Misty Lake about four years ago. She went out West to live and just seemed to disappear. Maybe her two brothers know something about her, but I never get to talk to them."

Addressing herself to Cecily, Mrs. Rumsey added, "I've seen wedding pictures of Susan. She resembles you so closely it's startling. You two must be related."

Cecily was so surprised she did not comment. Nancy asked quickly, "Mrs. Rumsey, does Susan have red hair?"

"Oh, yes. Lovely, too."

Nancy and the others exchanged excited glances! Could Susan be the red-haired stranger at Misty Lake?

Cecily smiled at the woman. "I'm trying to find out some information from the Waynes. It's very important. If the Wayne brothers return within the next few days, will you ask them to get in touch with me at Mrs. Hosking's in Misty Lake village?

Otherwise, I hope they will contact Niko Van Dyke, the singer."

"Do you know him?" Mrs. Rumsey asked. "I just love his records."

Cecily blushed. "We're engaged."

"Oh, you lucky girl!" Mrs. Rumsey exclaimed. "I wish you all the best."

Cecily thanked her, then Nancy expressed her appreciation for the woman's help and the four girls went off. They had lunch, then checked into the motel at which they had arranged to stay, and where Ned, Burt, and Dave would meet them.

Soon after Nancy and the others had rested, showered, and dressed, the Emerson College youths arrived. All were grinning, obviously happy at seeing their favorite dates. Cecily was introduced to the three boys.

"I've always wanted to hear Niko in person," said Ned, a handsome, dark-haired, athletic youth.

Burt was of medium height, husky and blond, while Dave was tall and rangy, with green eyes.

Amid much gaiety, the seven dined at a restaurant, where the boys were told of the mysteries Nancy was trying to solve.

Later, when they reached the theater, they found a mob of people already there, most of them in their teens or early twenties.

"It's a good thing we have reserved seats," Ned remarked.

Inside the theater the audience was shouting excitedly, and when the lights dimmed and the band came out, thunderous clapping started.

By the time Niko Van Dyke appeared on the stage, there was a standing ovation with screams and yells. The young musician turned around, and smiling broadly, bowed several times. When the pandemonium did not lessen, he held up his hand for silence. Finally the audience quieted down.

"Your fiancé sure is popular," whispered Bess to Cecily, who beamed.

Every number on the program drew wild acclaim, and after Niko had sung a second time, there was no holding down the teen-agers. They kept up continuous applause which was so loud that the last number on the program could hardly be heard above the din.

"How is Niko ever going to get out of this place without being mobbed?" Nancy leaned over to ask Cecily.

"A private car is always waiting for him and he's rushed off in a hurry. We're to go backstage and see him after the performance."

As the audience filed out, still in a delirious state, Cecily and her friends made their way to a door which led to the dressing rooms. A watchman unlocked it.

The group enthusiastically praised Niko for his

"Quick, Nancy! Crouch down!" the bandleader advised

fine performance. He thanked them, but added wearily, "It was a terrific session, but getting out of here is a real problem."

Everyone waited, hoping most of the audience would have left the sidewalk near the alley. But they were not to be cheated out of a close view of their favorite performer!

"I'll just have to chance it," Niko said finally. "Tonight two cars are waiting. Some of us will go in the first, and the rest in the second. We'll go to your motel first, girls, then decide what to do for the rest of the evening."

As the guard opened the stage door, the uproar began again. Cecily shrank back. Inadvertently, Nancy was the first one to leave the building, with Niko directly behind her. He grabbed her arm and guided her through the mob toward the first car parked in the alley.

The driver hopped out and quickly opened the rear door for Nancy and Niko. As soon as they were seated, Niko locked the doors and said to the driver, "Get us out of here!"

The car started slowly forward. "Quick, Nancy! Crouch down!" the bandleader advised, to keep the crowd from spotting them and stopping the car. The plan succeeded and they finally reached the street. The driver turned right, and when they had gone a block, Niko and Nancy sat up. The musician said, "Take us to the Stratford Motel."

At the next corner Nancy expected the driver to turn left. Instead, he went straight ahead. After three more crossings, she realized he was going far out of the way to the motel. She whispered this to Niko, who queried the driver. But the man merely said, "I know where I'm going!"

Suddenly panic seized Nancy. She whispered to Niko, "Is he your regular driver?"

"No," he answered. "Never gave it a thought. Why?"

The young sleuth spoke directly into Niko's ear. "I'm afraid we're being kidnapped!"

CHAPTER XV

Intensive Search

NIKO turned quickly and looked at Nancy, a stunned expression on his face. "Kidnapped!" he whispered back. "You mean it?"

Nancy nodded, murmuring, "I'll explain later. We'd better hop out at the next red light. If we get separated, let's meet at the motel."

Niko agreed and they watched for their chance, It came in about two minutes. As they reached a busy intersection, the light showed red and the driver stopped. Quick as a wink, Nancy and Niko were out of the car. They did not even take time to close the doors, but dashed left and right through the maze of stopped automobiles and ran in opposite directions down the cross street. Nancy found a cab and told the driver her destination. She hoped Niko had had as good luck as she had.

When her taxi pulled up in front of the motel she was relieved to see that he had just arrived.

Cecily, with the others, came to greet them in the lobby. She smiled but pretended to be hurt. "I thought you two had run off together!"

Niko did not smile. "Wait until you hear what happened!"

When he and Nancy finished the story, their friends sobered instantly. "Kidnapped!" cried Bess fearfully, while Cecily grew pale.

"Do you think those record pirates are behind this, Nancy?" George asked. "They may have found out you were investigating them and want you out of the way!"

"Yes," Nancy declared. "And furthermore, I think I was the one those men intended to hit with the rock at the cottage. Because the lights were dim they mistook Cecily for me."

Ned spoke up. "I don't like this whole thing. Nancy, you've risked enough danger."

"Those crooks probably trailed Nancy from Misty Lake," Dave declared.

"Dave!" Nancy cried out. "You've just given me an idea—about those mysterious Driscolls."

The others clamored to hear it. "I did have a hunch the brothers were doing some kind of secret work on a machine," Nancy went on. "Well, I now am very suspicious that they're mixed up in this record pirating. We girls heard cricket-like noises on the fraudulent record. That one, and many others, could have been made right near Misty Lake where the crickets are plentiful."

"Namely at Pudding Stone Lodge!" Ned guessed.

"Yes."

The others were astounded by Nancy's theory. She went on, "As soon as we get back to Misty Lake, I'm going directly to Neal Raskin's office again and see what I can find out."

"Right now, how about some ice cream?" Burt suggested.

The group went into the Stratford's soda shop. They selected a table in a far corner and Niko kept his back to other guests, hoping he would not be recognized.

"I'm sorry we've had such a hectic evening," he apologized.

Nancy chuckled. "I'm to blame too, Niko. So don't worry. We loved your show, anyway."

A short while later the young singer asked to be excused. "I admit I'm absolutely beat," he said.

The other boys insisted upon driving Niko to his hotel to be sure there were no more incidents. The girls waited in the lobby until Ned, Burt, and Dave returned.

Nancy and the cousins were delighted when the boys decided to accompany them to Misty Lake.

"We'll get a room at that Mrs. Hosking's

place." Ned grinned. "Nancy, you know we couldn't leave you with such a complicated and dangerous mystery to solve."

Soon afterward, the girls bade their friends good night. "See you in the morning," said Bess.

Nancy urged that they get an early start for the lake. "It's Sunday morning and there won't be too many cars on the road, so we can make good time. On the way, we can stop and go to church."

The others agreed, and after breakfast the boys and girls set off in the two cars. After attending church services, they stopped at a roadside restaurant for noontime dinner.

During the meal, the mystery and its various aspects became the sole subject of conversation. Ned chuckled. "Nancy, you certainly can get yourself involved in the most baffling cases. I'd like to bet that police chief at Misty Lake hasn't found out as much as you have!"

Nancy laughed. "What have I found out? Not much. I have only suspicions, I'm afraid!"

Nevertheless, when they reached Misty Lake village, Nancy discovered that Ned was right. Chief Stovall, who happened to be on duty at headquarters, admitted that he had learned nothing about the lake mysteries.

"I think I know who may have been bothering you at the cottage, though," he said. "A report reached my desk that a man had escaped from a mental institution and was hiding out in this area. But he's been recaptured."

Chief Stovall went on to say that he and his men had searched around the entire lake for clues to the phantom ship but had found nothing that warranted further investigation. "Are you positive, Miss Drew, that you really saw this—thing?"

For answer, Nancy said, "Mr. Henry Winch and some summer residents saw it before we did. I'm sure you have found him a very truthful citizen."

The police chief scratched his head. "Yes, we have."

Nancy smiled and changed the subject. "Do you know where Mr. Neal Raskin lives?"

"Yes. But if you're planning on seeing him, you can't do it before tomorrow. I happen to know he's out of town until then."

Nancy left headquarters and reported the chief's conversation to her companions. Ned said, "Well, Nancy, it looks as if you'll have to solve this mystery without the chief's help."

They stopped at Mrs. Hosking's to pick up Satin, the cat, and reserve a room for the boys. Then they all went down to the cottage. They ate supper in front of a roaring fire, and soon afterward the boys said good night.

"We'll meet you in the village tomorrow morning," Nancy told them. "I'll need your help in a sleuthing project."

Ned saluted. "We'll be ready and waiting."

When the young people met the following day, Nancy explained what she had in mind. She suggested that Ned call on the jobber.

"You might pretend you're interested in doing outside saleswork next summer, and get him talking about records in general and then Niko's latest one in particular."

Ned said he would be glad to do this and drove out to Raskin's office on the highway. When Ned returned somewhat later, he was flushed with excitement. "I picked up a great clue!" he said. "I'm sure I'm not mistaken. Raskin was the driver of the car that went off with Nancy and Niko!"

"What!" the others cried in unison.

Ned went on, "That's not all. He got a phone call while I was there. The person on the other end of the line talked so loud I could hear him. He said he was Webby. Isn't that the name of one of the men who was on the dock, Nancy, when you were hiding under it?"

"It certainly is," she replied. "Oh, Ned, your sleuthing has been marvelous. Do you know what this means? Raskin, Webby, and the Driscolls are partners in some scheme and I am sure it's pirating records!"

"Are you going to tell the police?" Bess asked.

"Not right now. I want more evidence before I talk to Chief Stovall or Detective Morton again," she said. "I think we should all go and make a thorough search of the Pudding Stone Lodge grounds for clues. But let's try to do it without being seen."

"That's going to be pretty hard," said George, "if they have spies around."

Nevertheless, everyone agreed to the idea and they went back to Misty Lake. The boys and girls watched intently as they walked through the woods to the cottage, but saw nobody.

The girls put on hiking shoes and the group set off. The plan was to circle the estate. The boys were to stay among the trees near the lane which led from the road to the lodge, go around the house, and make their way to the beach. Meanwhile, the girls would take the woods trail that led to the foot of the bluff below the stone house.

They separated. When the girls reached the area where they had heard the humming noise, they began an intensive search along the base of the incline for a hidden door that might lead underground to the lodge. The place was tangled with weeds and at this point sharply rocky.

"We'll have to tear these vines apart," George declared.

Suddenly the group was startled by children's shrieks from above. At once the girls raced up the path to the bluff. As they paused behind some bushes in an overgrown garden near the house,

they saw Vince Driscoll and the twins. He was toss-
ing each youngster in turn high into the air and
pretending that he wasn't going to catch them.
The little boy and girl looked terrified.

"We must do something!" said Bess.

Just then the agonized scream of a woman came
from the house!

CHAPTER XVI

Directions to a Treasure

As the woman's scream died away, Vince Driscoll set the twins on the ground and looked upward at the house. The four girls followed his gaze but could see no one at the windows. Who had screamed? Mrs. Driscoll? Or someone else?

Instinctively Nancy's eyes turned to the bull's-eye window. *Was* someone imprisoned in that room?

Vince now grabbed the children and rushed them into the house. Bess was so indignant she forgot to be fearful. "That's downright cruelty to children!" she said. "I think we should stop it!"

Nancy, George, and Cecily agreed, but George cautioned, "If we antagonize the Driscolls now, they'll never let us come back here."

The girls continued to speculate on the woman who had screamed. "It might even be that red-haired girl!" said Nancy.

"Then she certainly can't be in league with the Driscolls," said Cecily. "Oh, dear! I wish we could help her, and also find out if she *is* Susan Wayne."

Nancy was thinking the same thing. She put in words an idea which had been in her mind for some time. "I believe the twins are a key to some mystery involving the Driscolls. The red-haired girl knows it and they don't dare let her get away to tell it."

The others were speechless at first, then George said flatly, "I believe you're right, Nancy. But what can we do?"

Nancy felt that for the present the girls should continue their search. George suggested that since they were not far from the house, they might look again for the iron bird. She pointed to part of a broken stone bench, partially covered with weeds. "This place evidently was a garden at one time," she said. "Some ornamental bird might have been standing in it."

Cecily was eager to follow George's hunch, so the girls, trampling the tall grass, pulled up matted vines and kicked aside small loose stones to see if they were concealing any object.

Nancy had just pushed another stone out of the way, when the toe of her shoe hit something hard. She leaned over and saw that it was a protruding piece of rusty metal.

Excitedly she dug around it with the heel of her shoe. The other girls came to assist. George found a stout tree branch and began to use it like a spade. Finally the girls were able to pull the object out of the ground.

It was a tall graceful iron flamingo!

"The iron bird!" Cecily exclaimed, gazing at the rusted ornament.

The other three girls were excited. "Do you think the directions to your family fortune are still inside it?" Bess asked Cecily.

With almost loving care, Cecily ran her hands over the neck and body of the bird. She failed to find any kind of an opening.

"Let's try the legs," Nancy suggested.

There was no indication of an opening on the legs themselves, but under the bird's foot, the young sleuth thought she detected where a section had been soldered on.

"We can never get this piece off here," George stated. "Why don't we carry the bird to the cottage and work on it?"

Bess wondered about the advisability of taking the ornament off the property, but Cecily assured her that if it contained something belonging to her, she had every right to remove it, at least temporarily. So the four girls lifted the heavy iron flamingo and carefully descended toward the trail through the woods.

"Whew!" said Bess. "This weighs a ton. I wish the boys would show up and help carry it."

The three youths after an unsuccessful search of the grounds had returned to the cottage. When they saw the girls approaching they ran out to greet them.

"For Pete's sake, where did you unearth that thing?" Dave asked with a grin. "Out of an underground passageway?"

Nancy laughed and told the story. Cecily added that they wanted to pry open one of the bird's feet.

"We're exhausted," said Bess. "How about you muscle-men doing this little job?"

Removing the soldered wedge was rather a difficult task. Finally, however, the boys did accomplish it, and Ned reached into the small opening and pulled out a piece of paper folded over many times. When it was laid flat on a table it proved to be a fairly long letter.

Cecily began to read aloud: " 'From Simon Delaroy, your brother.' "

Cecily looked up excitedly. "This is to my great-great-grandfather—William!"

She continued to read:

" 'I am afraid Maryland will be invaded in the war that I know is coming, so, for reasons of safety, I have decided to divide the family fortune into two separate halves. If someone outside our family should find one half, the rest of the family will at least have the other. My dear William, your share I am putting in the corner cupboard in the kitchen. Besides money and some securities I am also including the family silver. This is what I have done: Broken our mother's locket in two and sent half to you. Perhaps the locket will prove to be a talisman, and, though the worst may happen in the next year or so, someday the two halves of the family may find each other again. We fear that mail from the North will be opened, so I have enclosed only a brief note about the fortune in the locket. By the way, I have hidden my portion of our family treasure in the beach house because that is a place very easily concealed.' "

As Cecily finished reading, everyone began to talk at once.

"It looks as if your mystery will be solved, Cecily!" said Bess. "And if this record racket is cleared up too, you and Niko can get married!"

Cecily beamed and said nothing would make her happier.

"But I'm completely puzzled about this beach house," she said. "We haven't seen any here. What do you make of it, Nancy?"

Nancy shook her head. "An ordinary beach house most certainly could not be concealed. This must have been a very special kind. Maybe we can find clues to it."

The young detective said she also wondered why anyone would choose a cupboard for a hiding place. "That, too, must have been a very special one."

"Why don't we just march up to the lodge and look for it?" George proposed. "After all, Mr. and Mrs. Karl Driscoll have invited us there, and even if that Vince doesn't want us around, apparently he isn't the boss."

Nancy was eager to follow this move. "It will give us a chance to look for the girl we think is Susan," she said. "If she *is* working for the Driscolls, she ought to be around the house at some time. But if she is their prisoner, the sooner we do something about that the better."

By now it was almost suppertime. The girls fixed a simple meal. The group ate quickly, then set off once more to Pudding Stone Lodge. When they reached it, the house was in complete darkness. No one answered their rings or knocking.

"Maybe they have left," Bess suggested. "If the Driscolls are crooks, they probably suspect the police are on their trail."

"I hate to think of those poor twins being dragged off." Bess sighed. "Especially by such awful relatives."

The young people waited awhile, but the place

remained silent and dark. Finally Nancy said, "We'll have to come back in the morning and see what we can find out."

The others agreed. They had had a long, hard day! As soon as they had eaten a snack at the cottage, the boys said good night and left.

Before she fell asleep Nancy's thoughts again turned to the twins. A hunch came to her. "It's fantastic," she admitted to herself. "I won't even tell the others until I'm sure!"

When the group assembled the next morning, Nancy announced a plan for trying to find out whether or not the red-haired girl was a prisoner at the lodge. Cecily was to play a prominent role by standing at a distance in sight of the house and pretending to be the other girl. Nancy would try to work things out so that she could call the attention of the Driscolls to Cecily. The girls synchronized their wristwatches, then all but Cecily went off. Part of the plan was for the three boys to remain hidden on the lodge grounds and trail anyone who came out of the house.

Nancy rang the front doorbell and Mrs. Driscoll came to answer it. She looked surprised but readily admitted the three girls.

"How are the children?" Nancy asked, smiling.

"Oh, they're fine. They both love it here." The woman did not offer to let the girls see the twins, however.

"We heard a woman's scream come from here yesterday afternoon," George spoke up. "Was anybody hurt?"

Mrs. Driscoll looked startled. "Oh, I guess you must have heard me. I thought I saw a mouse in the kitchen. They always frighten me."

The girls were dubious but did not continue the discussion.

Nancy spoke up, "Our main reason for coming back is that we picked up a clue regarding the iron bird. Do you mind if we look in the cupboards?"

"I guess it will be all right," Mrs. Driscoll said, but the girls thought she acted rather nervous.

She followed them into the kitchen and watched as Nancy opened the cupboard door. Only dishes, glassware, and some pots and pans were revealed. The young sleuth pulled over a step stool, climbed up, and examined the top shelf thoroughly. There was no sign that a secret door or sliding panel concealed a hidden treasure.

"Nothing here," Nancy said, climbing down.

They all walked into the dining room where there was a fireplace. The room had no real cupboard, but alongside the brickwork was a niche in which stood a beautiful vase.

"Are there any other cupboards downstairs?" Nancy asked, casually looking at her watch.

"No," the woman replied.

At that moment Karl Driscoll walked into the

room. He stared at the girls, then nodded curtly, looking annoyed at their presence. Nancy wondered if they had disturbed some project of his. As if lost in thought, she walked toward the window. Suddenly Nancy asked, "Who is that red-haired girl down on the beach? Do you know her?"

The question had an electrifying effect on the Driscolls. They rushed to the window and looked out over the bluff. Cecily was in plain sight below. Now she turned as if heading for the misty end of the lake. With a muttered excuse, Karl Driscoll fairly ran into the kitchen. The girls dared not follow, but they heard a door close softly and footsteps pounding down the cellar stairs.

Nancy continued to look out the window and in about two minutes she spotted two men on the beach—Karl Driscoll and his brother Vince! How had they reached it without her seeing them leave the house? "I'm sure now they use an underground passage," Nancy thought. The men started off on a run toward the misty end of the lake and disappeared around a bend. Cecily could no longer be seen.

With difficulty, Nancy kept calm. She was sure her ruse had worked! The other red-haired girl *was* being held in the house and the Driscolls thought she had escaped!

"Now to hunt for the prisoner!" Nancy thought.

CHAPTER XVII

The Mysterious Beach House

As Nancy wondered how she could get upstairs to investigate the room with the bulls'-eye window, she saw Mrs. Driscoll looking hard at her, Bess, and George.

"I think you've done enough searching," the woman said crisply. "You'd all better go now."

Nancy knew she could not force the issue. Disappointed, she and her friends thanked Mrs. Driscoll and went outside.

"I hope those two men didn't catch up with Cecily," Bess said worriedly.

George chuckled. "She had a good head start. I'm sure she doubled back and is safely locked in the cottage."

The girls lingered nearby, hidden among the trees. This was the spot where they were to meet the three boys, who came along a few minutes later.

"Any luck?" Nancy asked them.

Ned replied, "No one came out of the house."

Nancy explained what had happened and the boys gave low whistles. "Wow!" said Burt. "The Driscoll brothers really took the bait!"

"Yes," said Nancy. "But I wish we could have gone upstairs."

Suddenly Bess warned, "Ssh! Here come Mrs. Driscoll and the twins."

The six kept motionless in their hiding place. The woman did not seem to be searching for anyone, however. Yanking a child by each hand, she hurried down the bluff path and set off along the beach in the direction her husband and brother-in-law had taken.

"Now's our chance!" Nancy said. "If the girl is a prisoner in that house, we must set her free!"

She and the others hurried to the door. It was locked, as was the one to the kitchen.

Nancy turned to Ned and pointed out the bull's-eye window, which was open. "Do you think you can toss a stone through that window?"

Ned was sure he could. As the group moved through the woods toward the far side of the house, he began looking for a suitable stone.

Nancy rummaged through her handbag for a piece of paper on which to write a message. She did not find any, and the others confessed that they had neither paper nor pencil.

"It doesn't matter," said Nancy. "If the girl is locked in that room, she'll know the stone wasn't thrown by her enemies—there would be no reason for them to do so. I'm hoping she'll realize someone is trying to help her."

Ned stood far enough back, took careful aim, and threw the stone as if it were a high forward pass. It sailed neatly through the round opening! The group below waited tensely for a response. A few minutes went by in complete silence, and they began to despair. Maybe no one was in the room. Then suddenly the stone was tossed out the window!

Nancy was excited. "Someone *is* a prisoner in there!"

Burt spoke up. "I can't understand why the Driscolls didn't check the attic room before they rushed after Cecily."

Nancy replied, "My guess is that Karl was so excited at seeing the red-haired girl nothing else entered his mind except that his prisoner had escaped. He rushed down to the cellar, found Vince, and dashed to the beach through a secret tunnel. But, in the meantime, Mrs. Driscoll probably was suspicious, and went to the attic to find out. When she discovered the other red-haired girl still there, she grabbed the twins, and went to warn the men—"

She stopped speaking abruptly at the sound of

voices in the woods below. In a short while the hidden group could see the three Driscoll adults and the twins coming back to the house. As they came nearer, the little boy cried out, "I wanted to play in the water!"

"Shut up, you brat!" Karl Driscoll said, slapping the boy hard.

The little girl began crying as she tried to comfort her brother. Mrs. Driscoll hustled them into the house and the men followed.

Nancy again thought of her secret hunch. "It's doubly important for us to get to Susan Wayne—or whoever the red-haired girl is—to learn if I'm right," she said to herself.

"I'd like to sock that guy!" Ned burst out, and the others nodded vigorously.

Then Nancy suggested that Bess, George, Burt, and Dave station themselves to watch the house from every angle. "Ned and I will first check on Cecily. Next, we'll drive to town and tell our story

to Chief Stovall. I hope he'll come and make an investigation."

The couple hurried off to get Ned's car. They found Cecily in the cottage, cautioned her to keep the door locked, and assured her they would tell her everything later. The trip to Misty Lake village did not take long. Chief Stovall was on duty. He listened patiently to Nancy's account, but was obviously skeptical. "Your evidence is pretty flimsy, Miss Drew," he said.

The young sleuth reddened but did not reply. Her blue eyes held a disapproving look, however, and finally the chief promised that he himself would come out with one of his men and look over the lodge premises.

"Please! Can't you come now?" she urged.

The chief smiled. "You are an impatient young lady. Well, I guess we can make it."

When the two cars reached the right-hand fork which led to Pudding Stone Lodge, Nancy suggested that the chief wait until she checked with her friends to find out what had happened at the lodge. But the watchers had nothing to report.

"No one has left the house," George announced.

"That's fine," said Nancy. "The police are ready to go in."

She and Ned ran back to the squad car and gave this news to the officers. "When we see you come out, we'll meet you here," Nancy said.

The six friends stationed themselves in an ever-green grove and peered out. They saw Karl Dris-coll open the door and readily admit the police. Nancy thought she detected a momentary look of fright on his face. Time dragged by. Finally the two officers came out. To Nancy's consternation, thay parted from the Driscolls on what seemed to be very pleasant terms.

Puzzled, the whole group made their way through the woods to the spot where the police car was waiting. Chief Stovall leaned out the window and addressed himself to Nancy.

"We didn't find a thing. We even broke into that locked attic room to be sure. No sign of any prisoner. Besides, those people don't seem in the least suspicious. Miss Drew, I feel that you may have overstepped in this situation. You know tres-passing is against the law. I warn you to stay away from the lodge. You've caused the Driscolls enough inconvenience."

Nancy was too embarrassed and crushed even to argue. Chief Stovall said that he and his man had searched every corner of the house from attic to cellar. "So I'm sure you all can spend the rest of your vacation here just having fun."

Despite the jolt to her spirits, Nancy politely thanked the chief for his time and effort, then the group said good-by. They were silent on the walk back to the cottage. Nancy's friends felt sorry for her—she had worked so hard to solve the mystery and now everything she had achieved seemed to be crashing into bits.

When they reached the cottage, Cecily was given a full account of the morning's adventures. Although disappointed, she tried hard to encourage Nancy. Bess coaxed the young sleuth to eat a good lunch, and by the time the sandwiches were finished, Nancy's interest in the case had been renewed.

She suddenly burst out, "I've a hunch that the Driscolls moved their prisoner to a different hiding place. The thing for us to do is find it!"

"That may be very difficult," said Dave. "Do you have an idea where it is?"

"Yes, I have. The beach house Simon Delaroy mentioned in his letter."

"But there isn't any beach house!" Bess pointed out.

Nancy reminded the others that Simon had said the beach house was easily concealed. "I've suspected for some time it's actually a room connected with the cellar of the lodge and has an opening onto the beach."

"And all *we* have to do is find it," George said wryly. "Well, I'm with you, Nancy. Let's not admit defeat yet."

The kitchen was tidied, then once more the six set off. Cecily had decided to stay at the cottage.

Suddenly Nancy mentioned the police chief's warning against their trespassing.

"Maybe we're okay," George spoke up. "When I was hunting up the history of the lodge, I kept right on up to the present time. A large part of the original Wayne estate has been sold, including beach rights, to the village of Misty Lake."

Nancy chuckled. "You mean that if anyone orders us off, we can counter by saying we know that the property has been sold?"

George grinned. "Work it anyway you like."

As they walked along, Burt asked, "If the police searched the lodge from attic to cellar, why didn't they find the beach house if it's connected to the cellar?"

"Because the entrance is concealed," Nancy replied. "When I was in that room in the cellar, I noticed a door behind a chest. I believe that it leads into what Simon called the beach house."

They reached the edge of the woods. Ned was in the lead. "Hold it," he said. "We're not going to do any searching now. Vince Driscoll is sitting on the beach facing the bluff. I'll bet he's guarding the place." The others agreed.

Although thwarted, they all were excited. Nancy's belief about a hidden room must be true! The young people waited awhile, but Vince showed no signs of leaving.

Finally the girls and their escorts returned to

the cottage. Frequently they took turns walking down to the lake front to look up at the Pudding Stone Lodge beach. Vince Driscoll was still there. At sundown they saw his brother Karl relieve him and take up the watch.

Nancy wondered if the phantom launch would appear, but it did not. As it grew darker, Karl produced a flashlight and kept moving it back and forth as he patrolled the beach.

"I'm convinced now that he's guarding the beach to keep us away," said Nancy. "I guess our only hope is to outwait him. I have an idea."

She suggested that they all join in singing and laughing, and then the boys would say in loud voices, "Good night! See you in the morning!" Instead of leaving, they were to take up a watch among the trees near the beach. "Alert us as soon as Driscoll goes away," Nancy requested.

The plan was carried out. The boys left and the girls turned out the cottage lights. They tried to remain awake but could not keep from dozing off.

About an hour later they were startled out of their sleep by loud pounding on the cottage door. Nancy was the first to reach it, and flung it open.

Dave stood there, out of breath and excited. "Hurry! The Driscoll brothers are loading a truck. We heard them say it's for a big delivery! This is our chance to catch those crooks red-handed!"

CHAPTER XVIII

The Chase

"You mean," Nancy said excitedly, "a delivery of illegal records?"

"I'm sure of it," said Dave. "We got close enough to hear Karl Driscoll say there's going to be a second delivery later—to Baltimore. After that, he said, the Driscolls, the children, and Susan would make their getaway."

"Susan!" Nancy echoed.

The girl detective was once more puzzled. What had Karl meant by getaway? Was the red-haired girl not a prisoner, but mixed up in the Driscolls' racket? Had Susan dropped the half locket? And what about the twins? Was Nancy's secret theory true?

Now she quickly outlined a plan to the others. This time, Cecily insisted on taking part.

"I think you boys should follow the truck," Nancy said. "We girls will watch the house."

"That's a good idea," Dave agreed.

"We may all have to do some chasing sooner or later," Nancy went on. "We'd better take both cars and hide them along the lane that leads to the main road."

They locked the cottage and hurried up to the two cars. Ned and Burt were waiting for them behind trees at the intersection of the road leading to Pudding Stone Lodge.

A minute later a truck pulled away from the stone house and roared down the road. Nancy and the others strained their eyes to see who was in it. As it lumbered past, they saw that the driver was Vince. Nancy identified the man beside him as Webby.

"Let's go, fellows!" Ned urged, and told Nancy that on the way the boys would telephone Detective Morton in Baltimore.

As soon as the youths' car was out of sight, Nancy drove the girls nearer the lodge, hid the car once more, and the four proceeded on foot. Nancy signaled a halt beneath a lighted open window on the second floor. "Listen!"

The girls could hear the twins crying. The little girl was begging plaintively for a story.

Mrs. Driscoll's annoyed voice floated down clearly, "Don't bother me! Go to sleep!"

The little girl asked, "Why are we dressed? We never go to bed with all our clothes on!"

The girls grew tense. This corroborated Dave's statement that the occupants were all leaving. "But how soon?" Nancy wondered. She must find Susan!

"Bess and George," whispered Nancy, "you keep spying on the lodge. If Mrs. Driscoll drives away with the children, follow her. If Susan is with them, George, give the owl signal whistle we use sometimes. Meantime, Cecily and I will investigate the beach."

Nancy did not dare use her flashlight. She and Cecily picked their way carefully down the wooded bluff to the bottom. She felt it was almost hopeless to hunt for a hidden door in the heavy growth of vines on the darkened hillside, but she was determined to try. Both girls carried on a long, tedious search.

Suddenly Nancy touched cold metal, then felt the outline of a door! Elated, she was just about to try pulling it open, when suddenly a voice nearby hissed, "Now I've got you right where I want you!"

Nancy and Cecily froze in fright. They expected to be grabbed, or be revealed in a flashlight's glow. But nothing happened! No one appeared!

The girls stared at the door, and now noticed dim light coming through a rounded opening at the top. They could not see in. The same voice went on, "Your brother ain't here to back you up, Karl, so you're goin' to account to me!"

Nancy and Cecily stood close together, holding hands. Their hearts were thumping. The voice was coming from just inside the secret door!

"Okay, Raskin. What's your beef?" Karl asked.

Neal Raskin! So he *was* mixed up in the Driscolls' racket!

"Why didn't you keep that snoopin', pryin' Nancy Drew from ruinin' our record game?"

In a whining voice Karl tried to defend himself. "I found this place for us, didn't I? When we discovered it was empty and we couldn't collect any reward for those kids, I rented it for our record factory."

Reward for the children! Nancy and Cecily stared at each other in bewilderment.

Karl went on, "Wasn't I the one that set up that sound movie of the phantom launch to scare off the summer residents and that Winch fellow?"

There was no answer, and Driscoll added, "I was watching from the attic the night Nancy Drew and the other girls came to that cottage. And later when I spotted her near here, I signaled to Vince over the intercom to stop the machinery in the beach house.

"That was a busy night for me. Susan Wayne had escaped. Vince and I caught her in the woods, tied her up, gagged her, and dragged her back to the lodge. On the way I heard footsteps and saw some girl climbing the slope. I pushed her from behind and she fell down. I guess she was knocked out because she didn't move. When I went back later to take a look, Nancy Drew was with her. So I rolled a big log down on the two of them."

"All right," said Raskin. "So you captured Susan Wayne because she found out too much about you three and the racket. But you still didn't stop that Drew dame."

"You messed up things yourself!" Karl retorted. "You try to kidnap her and Niko Van Dyke and they get out of the car and walk away!"

Raskin snorted indignantly. "How did I know she suspected they were being kidnapped?"

"I worked hard on this business," Karl insisted. "I even apologized when Vince ordered those girls away so they wouldn't get suspicious, and then bought that iron bird to fool them. When you told me the Drew girl's friends came to your office I tried to scare her away from Misty Lake. I locked her out on the roof and sent Vince flying over to wreck the cottage so they'd all go home. And just in case that didn't work, I had him put a hole in the canoe."

"But that didn't frighten off Miss Nancy Drew, either!" Raskin said angrily.

"Is it my fault she don't scare easy?" Karl asked.

"Even when Vince and I sneaked down to the cottage and threw a rock inside, she and her pals didn't leave."

"Yes, but what good did that do?" Raskin sneered. "That girl detective sure can put it all over you. She tricked you by makin' you think a red-haired girl on the beach was Susan and that she had escaped."

Karl admitted this, saying he had panicked and had not stopped to think. But his wife had, and found Susan still locked in the attic room. "So I moved her down here to the beach house and whistled for Vince to come back. I had a feeling Nancy Drew would get the police. But I fooled them plenty, so you can't say I haven't done anything."

Raskin complained, "We had a swell racket goin'. Now, thanks to those nosy girls, we got to stop it. After we get the load of records out tonight, we'll be out of business."

There was no conversation for a few minutes. Nancy and Cecily could hear boxes being shoved around. Finally Karl said, "This is the last box. We'll carry this up, load the truck—it'll be full— and take care of Susan later."

The two girls heard footsteps receding. When she was sure they had left the room, Nancy tried the door. It would not budge. She called Susan's name but there was no answer.

"Oh, we *must* get in there and save Susan!" Cecily said, as she and Nancy kept pushing and pulling on the door.

It had started to drizzle and instantly Nancy thought of slippery roads. She wondered how the boys were making out.

At that very moment Ned, Burt, and Dave had pulled into an all-night gas station. While the attendant filled up the tank, Ned rushed to a phone booth and called police headquarters in Baltimore, asking that Detective Morton be alerted about the Driscoll truck headed for the city.

Ned dashed outside, climbed behind the wheel, and resumed the pursuit. Vince's truck was not going very fast in the misty drizzle, so it was easy for the boys to catch up. Suddenly the truck turned into a bumpy side road, only one lane wide.

"Where do you suppose they're making this delivery?" Dave asked.

Burt replied, "I can't imagine."

It had begun to rain hard now and the poorly paved road was very slippery. On the left side was a deep ditch. Ned kept as far from it as possible.

Presently he slowed down at a sharp curve where a large sign warned:

Sound Horn

Go Slow

"Vince Driscoll didn't sound his horn," Dave pointed out.

"You can bet I'm not going to sound mine," Ned answered.

He had driven only a short distance beyond the curve when the trio saw the truck turning around in a widened place in the road. It started forward —straight for the boys!

"That guy's not going to stop!" Ned exclaimed, and began to back up. He negotiated the curve successfully, but had to go so slowly that the truck overtook them. It hugged the inside of the road and squeezed the boys' car toward the deep ditch.

Ned's car skidded, and swerved to the edge. He applied the brake, but it was hopeless. The next moment the car dropped backward and crashed into the ditch.

CHAPTER XIX

Captured!

THE truck roared away down the narrow road. Ned, Burt, and Dave had instinctively let their bodies go limp and were only badly shaken up when the car had plunged into the ditch.

They scrambled out and surveyed the situation. At first glance the boys were sure a wrecker would be needed to pull out Ned's car.

"It's going to be a long walk in the rain," Dave complained. "I'd like to get hold of that Vince Driscoll and let him have it!"

"I would too, but right now we're stuck," said Ned. "Let's try to get this bus out of here. First, I'll see if it still runs."

To his relief, the engine started at once. Ned climbed out and together the three athletes tried to shove the car onto the road. They found it was impossible to move it up the steep side of the ditch,

but in the glare of the headlights, Ned saw that the
ditch grew shallower a short distance ahead. Together, the boys pushed the car through the mud
and weeds until they reached this spot. Then, with
a mighty heave, they managed to get one front
wheel onto the pavement. A few minutes later the
car was back on the road.

The boys grunted in satisfaction. Burt remarked, "I never thought we'd do it. Well, let's
get those pirates!"

"I don't think there's much chance of that now,"
Ned said. "I'll stop back at the service station and
phone the Baltimore police."

When Ned pulled in, the attendant looked at the
boys in surprise, then at the mud-covered car.

"We were forced off the road," Ned explained.
"I'd like to use your phone again."

"Help yourself."

When Ned talked to a sergeant on duty, the
officer surprised him with some good news. "The
State Police nabbed those men in the truck.
They're being held at Sayreville."

"That's great!" Ned said. "Have they confessed?"

"They won't say a word. But we've got that load
of records."

Ned started to ask if anyone from the State
Police had gone to Pudding Stone Lodge. Then
the line went dead. He hurried outside and reported to the other boys.

"We'd better get back there pronto ourselves," Ned urged.

He jumped behind the wheel and drove off. Despite the heavy rain, they made good time to the cottage. No one was there and the boys were concerned about Nancy and her three friends.

"They must still be staking out the lodge," Burt suggested. "Let's go there and see if the second truck has gone yet."

When they reached the garage, it was empty. "The truck may be at the house getting loaded," Burt ventured.

Ned suggested that Dave go to town and notify Chief Stovall of what had happened and bring back help.

"To tell the truth," he added, "I'm worried about Nancy and the other girls. Burt and 1 will sneak up to the lodge and see if they're around."

Some time before this, Nancy, desperate to get into the beach house, had beamed her light around the hidden door. Finally she had found an old-fashioned key hanging under some vines. In a jiffy she unlocked the door, put the key back in place, and then quietly opened the door.

By the dim light inside, Nancy and Cecily saw a medium-sized room cluttered with machines, including a movie projector. Against one wall was a cot. On this a young woman with red hair lay bound and gagged.

"Susan!" Nancy and Cecily cried together, rushing to the girl's side.

Quickly they untied her. As she sat up, Susan stared at Nancy and Cecily. "I thought you were working for the Driscolls in some way!" she said in amazement. "That's why I ran each time I saw you."

"It's just the opposite," Nancy replied. "We're trying to capture them."

"You know about their racket?" Susan asked incredulously.

"Yes. Some friends of ours are trailing them right now. Susan, are you the daughter of Kenneth Wayne?"

"Yes!" was the amazed answer.

Cecily spoke up. "You look so much like me, Susan. I am sure you're a relative. Did you drop a bracelet with half a locket in an old abandoned rowboat?"

"Oh, is that where I lost it? I had been carrying the bracelet in my purse, but I was afraid the Driscolls would take that away from me, which they did later. I took out the locket—which I've had since I was a child—and kept it in my pocket."

Cecily now excitedly told the story behind her half locket. "I put yours and mine together, and they're a perfect fit," she concluded. "That's another reason I think we're related."

Susan cried out, "Oh, I'm so happy to have a

cousin like you. If we can only find your share of our family treasure!"

The girls begged Susan to continue her own story.

"The second time I escaped from the Driscolls I got as far as that old boat and thought maybe I could get away in it. The locket must have dropped out then. But that awful man, Vince Driscoll, and somebody they call Jake grabbed me and locked me up again."

"You poor girl!" Cecily said sympathetically. "But why are the Driscolls holding you prisoner?"

"It's a long story, but I'll try to explain."

"I think we're safe for a while," Nancy declared, "and we're dying to hear your story!"

Susan explained that she had been married four years earlier. Her name was now Talbot. "Pudding Stone Lodge belongs to my family. No one is left but me and my two brothers and they're in the Navy."

Nancy nodded, telling of their inquiries in Baltimore. "You had a special reason for coming here, didn't you?" Nancy asked gently.

Susan burst into tears. "Yes. The twins!"

Nancy's heart leaped. "Susan, am I right? Are you the mother of those adorable twins?"

"Y-yes, I am. And I won't leave here without them!"

Cecily stared at her cousin in utter amazement.

"But why do the Driscolls have them, and claim the children as theirs?"

"It's complicated, but I'll tell you as quickly as I can," said Susan. "When I was married, my husband and I moved out to the Middle West. A little over a year ago, when Kathy and Kevin were two years old, my husband and I took them on a camping trip. One night, when the children were asleep in the tent, and my husband and I were sitting a little distance away near the road, a crazy driver came careening along, lost control of the car, and ran right into Steve and me."

"How horrible!" Nancy murmured.

Susan went on to say from then on, the whole thing had been a nightmare. "I guess the driver was afraid the accident would be traced to him. Someone found us and took us to a hospital. Unfortunately, we had no identification on us."

Susan choked up. "My darling husband died. I was unconscious a long time and did not regain my memory or health for nearly a year. Then I asked for my children. No one knew anything about them. The only explanation I could think of was that either the hit-and-run driver—or someone else who came along later—stole all our things and took the children. I reported this to the police, but they could find no trace of the twins."

"You must have been frantic!" Cecily cried out.

"I was. But one day I saw a picture in a newspaper of two acrobatic brothers. With them were twins who looked like Kathy and Kevin. I decided to investigate on my own and went to the town mentioned in the newspaper. I found out where the acrobats, whose name was Driscoll, lived, but when I went there I found the Driscolls and the wife of one of them had left with the twins. The only clue the landlady could give me was that they had mentioned a place called Pudding Stone Lodge!"

Susan said the woman had remembered that the twins' small trunk had borne the name of the lodge on the lid. "I was sure it was the same trunk I'd had as a child," Susan added. "I had given it to Kathy and Kevin. Pudding Stone Lodge was my childhood home."

Nancy and Cecily listened with bated breath as Susan continued her story. She had immediately started to Misty Lake. If she discovered her children at Pudding Stone Lodge, she intended to go to the local police for help.

"And did you see your twins?" Cecily asked.

Susan nodded sadly. "When I reached the lodge, no one answered my ring. The door was open and I was so eager I walked in. As I stood in the hall I heard loud arguments coming from the living room. It all concerned the cutting of illegal records. Suddenly I caught sight of Kathy and Kevin at the top of the stairs. I started up, but Vince

Driscoll discovered me. Evidently he was afraid I would go to the police about what I had heard, and he and his brother Karl tied me up and kept me gagged most of the time. Once I was able to scream, but it didn't help. Another time when my hands were free, I tossed back a stone someone pitched through the window."

"But Eddie at the soda shop says you ordered a record," Nancy said. "When and why did you do that?"

Susan explained that when she had first arrived in Misty Lake she had gone into the soda shop to inquire if anyone was living at the lodge. Eddie had been playing Niko's record and she had ordered one to give him a little business.

"Everything is becoming clearer now," Nancy remarked. "But I wonder how the Driscolls got hold of your children. They certainly don't act as if they did it for love!"

"That should be cleared up when the police arrest the Driscolls," Cecily suggested.

Nancy started. "We'd better go rescue the children!" she urged. "I was so interested in Susan's story that I forgot Karl and Raskin are coming back for her."

Hoping to avoid the men, the three girls hurried up the passageway from the beach house to the cellar of the lodge. Fortunately, the chest was still pushed aside, and they opened the door easily.

The girls made their way through the cellar and up the stairway to the kitchen. Hearing voices in the front hall they tiptoed through the darkness and Susan pushed open the swinging door that led to the hall. Mrs. Driscoll was there with the twins. All three were dressed, ready to leave the house.

Susan rushed forward impulsively and cried out, "They're my babies. You can't take them away!"

At that very moment Karl Driscoll opened the front door. He darted forward and grabbed Susan in an iron grip!"

Nancy and Cecily, who had waited in the kitchen, were about to rush forward and help the girl, when the back door opened. The next thing they knew, powerful arms engulfed them.

"You snoopin' busybodies!" Raskin's voice snarled in Nancy's ear. "This is the last time you're goin' to get in our way!"

The young sleuth struggled hard, but she was no match for the muscular man. Cecily had already been overpowered by a heavy six-foot stranger.

"We'll tie 'em good this time so they'll stay put," Raskin ordered. "Get busy, Jake!"

Apparently prepared for such emergencies, the two men pulled heavy cords from their pockets and tightly bound the girls.

Karl Driscoll dragged in Susan, who was also

tied up, and the three girls were forced roughly down the cellar stairs, through the passage, and into the beach house. Raskin locked the cellar door from the inside and pocketed the key. Jake swung open the exit to the beach. As the heavy door closed behind the men and was locked from the outside, Karl rasped, "You girls will never see daylight again!"

CHAPTER XX

A Rewarding Hunch

WHEN Raskin, Karl, and Jake dragged the girls away, Mrs. Driscoll grabbed the twins by the hand and pulled them out the front door. As they stepped onto the porch, Bess and George ran up. The woman attempted to brush by them, but George caught hold of Kathy. Kevin pulled loose and ran to Bess.

At that moment Ned and Burt dashed up the steps. "Where are Nancy and Cecily?" Ned asked.

Bess and George turned questioningly to Mrs. Driscoll. The woman's lips tightened firmly and she glared at the young people.

"The bad men took the pretty ladies to the cellar!" Kevin sobbed.

"The door is in the kitchen," George called as Ned and Burt raced into the house. They dashed down to the cellar and ran along the passageway.

It took only a minute for them to break down the door at the end.

"Ned! Burt!" Nancy and Cecily exclaimed when the boys burst into the beach house.

"Oh, Ned," Nancy cried, "I've never been so glad to see you!" Quickly she introduced the boys to Susan and told them the high points of her story.

As soon as the ropes had been removed from the girls, Susan ran to the door. "I must get my babies!" she declared.

By the time the five young people reached the front hall, they found Dave, Chief Stovall, and two policemen there. With them, handcuffed together, were Karl Driscoll, Neal Raskin, and the man called Jake. Bess had the twins by the hand while George firmly held Mrs. Driscoll's arm.

"We found these men trying to escape in a boat," Chief Stovall told Nancy, "but they refuse to talk. Perhaps you can help us."

Susan ran up to the children and put her arms around them. Before she could speak, the little girl said, "Are you Mommy?"

"Yes, darling," Susan said gently. "Come into the living room with me and I'll tell you all about it."

The little boy and girl smiled happily. "I'm glad," Kathy said shyly. "You're nice!"

Bess and George were amazed by this revelation

and overjoyed at the happy reunion. When Susan
and the twins had left, Nancy told Chief Stovall
the conversation she and Cecily had overheard in
the beach house. "I'm sure you'll find a load of
counterfeit records in the truck outside."

"Good for you, Miss Drew!" the chief said.
"You're an excellent detective and I apologize for
not taking your reports more seriously. Now tell
me about these children."

Nancy repeated Susan's story. "I don't know
how the Driscolls got the children," she admitted,
"but I suspect it was done illegally."

"Well, Driscoll, would you like to tell us or
shall we book you on a kidnapping charge?" the
chief said sternly.

Mrs. Driscoll spoke up. "Tell him, Karl. We
didn't know the twins had a mother living. It was
all a terrible mistake." She sank into a chair and
hid her face in her hands.

All the fight seemed to have gone out of Karl
Driscoll. He explained that he and his wife had
discovered the children at the edge of a campsite
one morning over a year before. There was no
one else around and they decided the twins had
been abandoned.

"We had been talking about using some children in the acrobatic act my brother Vince and I
had," he went on. "So we decided to train these
youngsters, just sort of informally adopted them.

The act didn't work out very well though, and a few months ago we decided to see if we could find the children's family and maybe collect a reward.

"The name Pudding Stone Lodge was burned into the top of a little trunk we found with the kids. I made some inquiries and learned of such a place on Misty Lake, so we came here. It was empty, but it looked like a good place for another project of ours, so I rented it. We were getting along okay until these busybody girls moved into that cottage."

"But what happened to the Talbots' car and all their luggage?" Nancy asked.

"We had to have money to take care of the kids," Karl replied sullenly. "We sold the car and the rest of the stuff."

"Driscoll," the chief said sternly, "you could not possibly have believed that those children were abandoned with the car and the luggage there. There's plenty you'll have to clear up for us. You come along now and join your pals in jail." The policeman led the four prisoners away.

"I want to thank you young ladies for helping rid Misty Lake of these disreputable characters," the chief said, "and solving the mystery of the phantom launch. Please say good night to Mrs. Talbot for me and tell her I'm delighted she has found her children."

A few minutes later Susan came into the room,

a happy smile on her face. "The twins are in bed," she announced. "They have really taken all this excitement very well."

"Do sit down, Susan," Nancy urged, "and clear up a few more puzzles for us. Did you try to signal from the bull's-eye window?"

"Oh, did you see me? My hands were tied and I was gagged, but I managed to get hold of a small mirror and move it in the sunlight. But Mrs. Driscoll caught me and took the glass away."

Susan continued, "They untied me and removed the gag when they brought me food, but one of them always stayed to guard me. One evening Vince was called away and I was left alone for a few minutes. He had taken the lamp, but I still had my handbag and got a flashlight from it. I signaled from the window, then with my nail file managed to push the key out of the lock, and pull it under the door with my fork. I escaped and ran into the woods but they caught me again."

"That's the night I saw you and called to you," Nancy put in. "But we know now you were too frightened to trust anybody."

Susan nodded, shivering a little. Then she brightened and turned to Cecily. "But I haven't forgotten that you have the other half of my locket and we're cousins! My father told me the story of the Delaroy brothers, our great-great-grandfathers, and how Simon's share of the family fortune was found in the beach house after the war. But Dad never knew what had happened to William."

Enthusiastic, Susan suggested that all the girls stay at the lodge and search for Cecily's treasure. They agreed.

Ned stood up. "I think we fellows had better go. If you girls are going to stay here, perhaps we can sleep at the cottage."

"Of course," said Cecily, and Nancy added, "Come back early in the morning. We'll all have breakfast together and then hunt for the treasure!"

Bess and George went with the boys and soon returned with overnight things for the four girls. It seemed they had just fallen asleep when they were awakened by a pounding on the front door. It was morning! They scrambled into their clothes and ran downstairs. There were Ned, Burt, and Dave—and Niko was with them!

"I wanted to find out what was going on here so I drove down after my performance last night," he explained. The girls welcomed him eagerly.

"We'll have breakfast ready in a jiffy!" Bess promised.

"I'm interested in Karl Driscoll's phantom launch," Ned remarked. "While you girls are rustling up the food, we fellows will go down to the beach house and take a look at his equipment."

When the boys returned a half hour later, an

appetizing meal of melon, bacon and eggs, toast and milk was ready.

"Did you find out exactly how Karl made the phantom launch appear?" Nancy asked.

"Yes. It is an ingenious arrangement of wires, sound projector, and a film clip. The picture was projected through the hole in the door onto the mist which gave it that eerie appearance. No wonder he had everyone around here scared silly!"

"All but Nancy!" Bess reminded him proudly.

"None of you really believed it was real," Nancy insisted. Then she said, "I vote we look right now for Cecily's treasure. It *must* be hidden around here some place!"

"Where shall we start?" George asked briskly.

Nancy replied that she had been mulling over the location of the cupboard mentioned in Simon's note. She had come to the conclusion that the present dining room could have been the old kitchen because it had the largest fireplace.

"When Simon wrote that he had hidden the treasure in the kitchen cupboard, it sounded too easy. The cupboard must have been camouflaged in some way. So I think we should investigate that niche where the vase stands."

"Lead on, Detective Drew!" Ned urged. "What shall we tear down first?"

Nancy smiled and turned to Susan. "Would you

mind if we take out the paneling below the shelf?"

"Go ahead!" Susan replied. "I can't wait to see if the treasure is there!"

The boys got tools from the cellar and carefully removed the wood panels from the wall beneath the niche. Rough plaster was revealed.

Nancy knelt and examined it. "I'm sure there's more wood under this plaster!" she said. "Let's take it off."

Under her direction, Ned and Niko chipped off the plaster. "There's a door here!" Niko called excitedly.

The young people gathered around breathlessly while Niko pried open the door. The space beyond was filled with packages.

"There's your family treasure, Cecily!" Niko said, straightening up and putting an arm around his fiancée.

"Oh, I can't believe it!" she exclaimed.

Ned and Burt dragged the bundles out and helped Cecily open them. There was one box filled with gold coins, a package of old securities, and piece after piece of beautiful silver.

"I wonder if the securities are worth anything now," Cecily remarked when she had spread everything out on the dining table.

Ned whistled. "Even if they're not, you have a fortune there in gold!"

Susan threw her arms around Cecily and said,

"Oh, I'm so glad you have your part of the family treasure!"

"Now Niko and I can get married!" Cecily beamed. "And it's all due to you, Nancy! You trapped the record pirates and found the fortune!"

"And helped me get back Kathy and Kevin," Susan said.

"I had a lot of assistance from Bess and George and the boys," Nancy said modestly.

"I have an idea," Niko spoke up. "'Cecily, why don't you and Susan combine your family resources? You can use some of your money to develop your property as a summer resort. You can build a dance pavilion out on the old picnic grounds and the Flying Dutchmen will provide the music!"

"That's wonderful, Niko!" Susan agreed. "And we'll restore the garden and install the iron flamingo in its old location!"

While the others were planning excitedly, Nancy was wondering wistfully when another mystery would come her way. She was to find out soon, upon discovering *The Message in the Hollow Oak*.

Cecily, meanwhile, had slipped from the room. She returned with the locket and whispered to Susan. When the girl smiled and nodded, Cecily raised her hand for silence.

"Listen, everybody," she said. "Susan and I want Nancy to have a memento of this adventure.

We're going to have the locket repaired and hope she will wear it and think of the cousins she has united through her detective work!"

"Hear! Hear!" Bess, George, and the boys cheered and applauded.

Nancy smiled, though her eyes were filled with happy tears. "Thank you both. I'll never, never forget you or the clue of the broken locket!"

JURASSIC PARK ™

THE RIDE

YOU'LL WISH IT WAS JUST A MOVIE.

COMING SUMMER '96

NIVERSAL STUDIOS HOLLYWOOD

For more information on Universal Studios Hollywood Vacations call (800) 337-5072.

Order Form

Own the original 56 thrilling
NANCY DREW MYSTERY STORIES®

In *hardcover* at your local bookseller OR
simply mail in this handy order coupon and start your collection today!

Mail order form to   PUTNAM PUBLISHING GROUP/Mail Order Department
390 Murray Hill Parkway, East Rutherford, NJ 07073

ORDERED BY
Name _____

Address _____

City & State _____ Zip Code _____

Please send me the following Nancy Drew titles I've checked below
All Books Priced @ $4.95.

AVOID DELAYS   Please Print Order Form Clearly

☐	1	Secret of the Old Clock	448-09501-7	☐ 29	Mystery at the Ski Jump	448-09529-7
☐	2	Hidden Staircase	448-09502-5	☐ 30	Clue of the Velvet Mask	448-09530-0
☐	3	Bungalow Mystery	448-09503-3	☐ 31	Ringmaster's Secret	448-09531-9
☐	4	Mystery at Lilac Inn	448-09504-1	☐ 32	Scarlet Slipper Mystery	448-09532-7
☐	5	Secret of Shadow Ranch	448-09505-X	☐ 33	Witch Tree Symbol	448-09533-5
☐	6	Secret of Red Gate Farm	448-09506-8	☐ 34	Hidden Window Mystery	448-09534-3
☐	7	Clue in the Diary	448-09507-6	☐ 35	Haunted Showboat	448-09535-1
☐	8	Nancy's Mysterious Letter	448-09508-4	☐ 36	Secret of the Golden Pavilion	448-09536-X
☐	9	The Sign of the Twisted Candles	448-09509-2	☐ 37	Clue in the Old Stagecoach	448-09537-8
☐	10	Password to Larkspur Lane	448-09510-6	☐ 38	Mystery of the Fire Dragon	448-09538-6
☐	11	Clue of the Broken Locket	448-09511-4	☐ 39	Clue of the Dancing Puppet	448-09539-4
☐	12	The Message in the Hollow Oak	448-09512-2	☐ 40	Moonstone Castle Mystery	448-09540-8
☐	13	Mystery of the Ivory Charm	448-09513-0	☐ 41	Clue of the Whistling Bagpipes	448-09541-6
☐	14	The Whispering Statue	448-09514-9	☐ 42	Phantom of Pine Hill	448-09542-4
☐	15	Haunted Bridge	448-09515-7	☐ 43	Mystery of the 99 Steps	448-09543-2
☐	16	Clue of the Tapping Heels	448-09516-5	☐ 44	Clue in the Crossword Cipher	448-09544-0
☐	17	Mystery of the Brass-Bound Trunk	448-09517-3	☐ 45	Spider Sapphire Mystery	448-09545-9
☐	18	Mystery at Moss-Covered Mansion	448-09518-1	☐ 46	The Invisible Intruder	448-09546-7
☐	19	Quest of the Missing Map	448-09519-X	☐ 47	The Mysterious Mannequin	448-09547-5
☐	20	Clue in the Jewel Box	448-09520-3	☐ 48	The Crooked Banister	448-09548-3
☐	21	The Secret in the Old Attic	448-09521-1	☐ 49	The Secret of Mirror Bay	448-09549-1
☐	22	Clue in the Crumbling Wall	448-09522-X	☐ 50	The Double Jinx Mystery	448-09550-5
☐	23	Mystery of the Tolling Bell	448-09523-8	☐ 51	Mystery of the Glowing Eye	448-09551-3
☐	24	Clue in the Old Album	448-09524-6	☐ 52	The Secret of the Forgotten City	448-09552-1
☐	25	Ghost of Blackwood Hall	448-09525-4	☐ 53	The Sky Phantom	448-09553-X
☐	26	Clue of the Leaning Chimney	448-09526-2	☐ 54	The Strange Message in the Parchment	448-09554-8
☐	27	Secret of the Wooden Lady	448-09527-0	☐ 55	Mystery of Crocodile Island	448-09555-6
☐	28	The Clue of the Black Keys	448-09528-9	☐ 56	The Thirteenth Pearl	448-09556-4

ALL ORDERS MUST BE PREPAID

_____ Payment Enclosed

_____ Visa

_____ Mastercard-Interbank #

Postage and Handling Charges as follows

$2.00 for one book

$ .50 for each additional book thereafter

(Maximum charge of $4.95)

Card # _____

Expiration Date_____

Signature_____
(Minimum Credit Card order of $10.00)

Merchandise total   _____

Shipping and Handling _____

Applicable Sales Tax   _____

Total Amount   [_____]
(U.S. currency only)

Order Form
New revised editions of
THE BOBBSEY TWINS®

In *hardcover* at your local bookseller OR
simply mail in this handy order coupon and start your collection today!

Mail order form to: PUTNAM PUBLISHING GROUP/Mail Order Department
390 Murray Hill Parkway, East Rutherford, NJ 07073

ORDERED BY

Name _____

Address _____

City & State _____ Zip Code _____

Please send me the following Bobbsey Twins titles I've checked below.
All Books Priced @ $4.95

AVOID DELAYS Please Print Order Form Clearly

☐ 1. Of Lakeport   448-09071-6   ☐ 5. At Snow Lodge   448-09098-8
☐ 2. Adventure in the Country 448-09072-4   ☐ 6. On a Houseboat   448-09099-6
☐ 3. Secret at the Seashore   448-09073-2   ☐ 7. Mystery at Meadowbrook 448-09100-3
☐ 4. Mystery at School   448-09074-0   ☐ 8. Big Adventure at Home 448-09134-8

Own the original exciting
BOBBSEY TWINS® ADVENTURE STORIES
still available:

☐ 13. Visit to the Great West   448-08013-3
☐ 14. And the Cedar Camp Mystery   448-08014-1

ALL ORDERS MUST BE PREPAID   Postage and Handling Charges as follows

_____ Payment Enclosed $2.00 for one book

_____ Visa $ .50 for each additional book thereafter

_____ Mastercard-Interbank #   *(Maximum charge of $4.95.)*

Card # _____   Merchandise total   _____

                                           Shipping and Handling   _____
Expiration Date _____
                                           Applicable Sales Tax   _____
Signature _____
Minimum Credit Card order of $10.00)   Total Amount   ┌──────────┐
                                           (U.S. currency only)   └──────────┘

The Bobbsey Twins® series is a trademark of Simon & Schuster Inc.,
and is registered in the United States Patent and Trademark Office.

Please allow 4 to 6 weeks for delivery.